An original dramatisation
produced by RT

GW00994000

'part le Carré, part Graham Greene'
—*Independent*

'Ireland's best-kept secret: Philip Davison is one of our great contemporary writers.'
—**Bob Geldof**

'Davison never fails to surprise, compel and intrigue with dry philosophy and grim wit . . . [He] shares Beckett's knack for making the down-at-heel appear surreal.'
—**Times Literary Supplement**

'Chilly, elegant and disconcertingly comic. Rather like a collaboration between two notable Green(e)s – Graham and Henry – and quite safely described as original.'
—**Literary Review**

'Davison writes with the intelligence and intent of a James Lee Burke, flecked with the mordant wit of a Kinky Friedman.'
—*Arena*

'Sharp. Funny. Hip. Learned. Surprising. . . Ireland's equivalent of Graham Greene with a dash of Le Carré and the readability of Len Deighton.'
—**Evening Herald**

'a gem of a writer . . . Davison's lean and ultra-minimalist style evokes an atmosphere that is quite surreal . . . He has a sparse and strangely matter-of-fact style of writing that gives full value to every word and act.'
—*Irish Times*

'As flawed heroes go, Harry Fielding must rank among the best of them.'
—**Irish Independent**

Quiet City

First published in 2021 by Ely's Arch
An imprint of Liberties Press
Dublin, Ireland
elysarch.com
libertiespress.com

Distributed in the United Kingdom by
Casemate UK
Oxford, UK
casematepublishers.co.uk

Distributed in the United States and Canada by
Casemate IPM
Havertown, Pennsylvania
casemateipm.com

Copyright © Philip Davison, 2021
The author asserts his moral rights.
ISBN (print): 978-1-912589-11-1
ISBN (e-book): 978-1-912589-12-8

2 4 6 8 10 9 7 5 3 1
A CIP record for this title is available from the British Library.
Cover design by Baker @ bplanb.co.uk
Printed in Dublin by Sprint Print

Quiet City

Philip Davison

Turn the key deftly in the oiled wards,

And seal the hushed casket of my soul.

from *To Sleep*, by John Keats

1

Richard Meadows

1

When Richard Meadows' wife told him he was showering too noisily he knew he had entered a new phase in his life. It wasn't his singing, because he didn't sing in the shower. There was the odd hum, but nothing that could be heard above the sound of water falling from the showerhead.

He shut off the water, stepped out onto the tiles, and put his head around the door. 'What?'

'You didn't hear?' said Gloria. Her eyes were wide and perfectly round.

'I heard,' said Richard. He looked at his wife with blank amazement. It was the actual business of showering that was too loud for Gloria's ears. She no longer admired him. That much he knew. However, Richard had come to believe that admiration might separate from love and be a more fickle thing.

On Monday morning last, Gloria had discovered the puny remains of one bar of soap her husband had melded with a new bar of soap to form something that closely resembled a fried egg, and she had flown into a rage. Richard had been able to deal with the soap incident. He could see how soap-melding might annoy a person, whatever the degree of familiarity. This complaint concerning his late-afternoon shower was of a different order. Richard could shower any time of the day now that he was doing just the occasional piece of consultancy work. This was a searing afternoon attack. It was significant that Gloria had delivered the same round-eyed look of contempt when she spoke on the topic of his strategy for ageing – which, admittedly, was to have no strategy at all.

The rebuke was delivered from the fan-ribbed Deco armchair that was positioned by the bedroom window. Gloria had taken to sitting on this chair in her pyjamas. She would rise early from their bed, then sit and gaze vacantly at the street below. She had bought this chair in an antique shop in Francis Street a year after the couple had married. It was an anniversary present from her husband. She chose it, and paid for it, and he reimbursed her. This he later regretted, as it made the chair something less than a present.

Richard dried himself in a stupor. Gloria changed into her clothes with a series of angry jerks, and left the apartment. In challenging times Richard issued audible warnings and kindness, but in a whisper. Recently, these whispers came with a soothing coda. He would address himself by name and counsel patience and kindness to himself. However, on this occasion there was no such warning, and no soothing words. In his state of undress he stood and stared at the empty chair. A cold, burning sensation travelled up his spine and across his shoulder blades. He shivered under the acid mantle Gloria had thrown on him. There was the vague expectation of a heart attack.

Richard turned the chair on its side to get it out through the bedroom door. He waltzed it down the hall, out onto the landing and into the lift. It was strangely empowering to sit in it for the descent to the basement car park. He felt he was occupying a dark and fabulous three-dimensional metaphor that saw him, a modest under-achiever, properly damned. He splayed his fingers and rubbed his palms on the arm-rests. He thought he might laugh like a madman, but the journey was short and the gong sounded. The door slid back, and the voice announced that he and the chair had arrived at 'Parking'.

It was difficult to get the chair into the dumpster. Gloria would have been impressed to see the effort he put in. In an earlier life she had been mightily taken with Richard and had fallen in love a little when, from a standing position, he had leapt over a college tennis net to be at her side. He was attentive and intelligent. This she expected from an engineering student, but she had, in particular, been attracted to his athleticism, and to his embarrassment at his good health and cleanliness.

Richard lifted the armchair high in the air and hoiked it over the lip of the dumpster with a great guttural groan. He stepped back and saw that the lumpish thing protruded and sat cockeyed on its bed of rubbish. He had always liked the chair, but the service it provided had to end. A line in the sand had to be drawn. A signal had to be sent.

He had an overwhelming urge to jump into the dumpster himself. It made no sense, but he did it anyway. He ran at the big bin in a most athletic manner, attempted a back-flip, but instead twisted clumsily over the lip and fell into the chair at a bad angle. He injured his shoulder on impact and the bed of rubbish collapsed. He was tipped face down with a violent jolt, but Richard was already intoxicated by his own irrational behaviour. He sprang to his feet, tumbled out of the bin, military fashion, and nearly fainted with the pain Gloria's chair had inflicted. Regardless, he set about covering his handiwork with scraps of cardboard.

He got into his car to watch. Soon the bin-men appeared at the electric gate. When they pulled away in their lorry he decided to follow. His injury had him listing at the steering wheel, but he wasn't bitter. This whole business was about change. In particular, it was about ageing. General physical decline had to be faced with noble contempt. Gloria wasn't attuned to the concept. She wasn't signalling that together they might be ennobled – which was why her beloved chair was on its way to the city dump.

Richard followed the lorry because he felt he had made a mistake – in ditching the chair, that is, not in jumping in after it. He wanted it back. He wanted the chair there in the bedroom with Gloria.

The bin-men had one last collection before going to the dump. The heavy loads that went in on top of the armchair were a torture for Richard, and now he realised that the sour, fishy stink was coming from his person as much as from the mother-ship. He wanted to go to some dark corner and quickly drink a bottle of wine, but that was most un-engineering of him. He determined he should stick to the task of retrieving the chair. How easily he had succumbed to a better view of things, he noted.

The lorry flew through the tip-gates with Richard's car close on its tail. The man in the hut showed no interest. The bin party went directly to the tip-head. Richard parked by a cluster of empty oil drums, got out and made his way to the action. It was near closing time. A bulldozer with porcupine wheels was idle, high on the refuse slope above. Scraps of paper and plastic sheeting caught in the netting trembled in a light evening breeze. The gulls were undisturbed by the heavy chugging of the lorry's engine and the surge of hydraulics. Richard took a moment to acknowledge the appropriateness of this latest three-dimensional metaphor, only to find he had misjudged the speed at which the dumping would be done. It was all over by the time his presence registered with the crew.

'Are you all right there, boss?' the bin captain asked.

'Yes,' said Richard. 'Thank you. I was just looking for something.'

'In there?'

'Yes.'

'What is it you want?'

'You see that chair . . . ?'

'You want that chair?'

'I do. It's mine. My wife's, that is. It went in by mistake.'

'By mistake?'

'It shouldn't have gone in.'

'Something wrong with you?' the captain asked. Richard took offence, but then realised the man was indicating his hunched shoulder.

'Ah. Yes. Banged it. Stupid really.'

'You want us to get the chair?'

'Would you?'

They didn't seem to mind that he stank of fish. Didn't seem to care. When the job was done Richard hooked a twenty out of his pocket and offered it.

'Good man,' cried the captain. The crew got in their lorry and drove off with a crunch of gears.

With the chair sticking out of the boot, Richard drove to the site entrance, where he found the gates locked and the security cabin deserted. He turned back. He had seen another gate that led to the adjacent recycling yard.

This gate was also locked. He switched off the engine, got out, scaled the fence and dropped into the recycling compound, more hunched then ever. There was a series of concrete trenches that housed long roller skips for public use. There was just one station wagon backed up to the furthest trough. A woman was unloading small, heavy goods. It was late in the day, but evidently she wasn't in a rush. Richard approached. Her appearance suggested she was thirty-nine or forty, but he was sure she was older. He was immediately attracted to her.

'Hello.'

'Hello,' she said. Her tone exactly matched his.

'You didn't happen to notice if there is a security man on the gate you came in?'

'Yes,' she replied. 'There is.'

'Oh good. It's just I got locked in next door.'

'Really?' She looked at him without seeming to judge – which, under the circumstances, set Richard rocking on his heels. He thought he recognised her. Was she one of Gloria's friends? No. The face came out of his distant past. Was this Virginia Coates? Virginia Coates was his childhood love. Could it really be her? What were the chances? He blamed his inability to definitively identify her on his psychological and physical trauma. If it *was* her, she didn't recognise him.

'Want a hand with that stuff?'

'I'm all right,' she said. 'Nearly done.'

It was mostly scrap metal she was dumping. Small engine parts – all of which Richard was able to name. There were also coils of old electric cable and crusted tins of paint.

'He's dead,' the woman declared robustly, but with a mischievous glance. 'I'm clearing out the garage.'

Virginia Coates was mischievous and disarmingly direct. It was odd how young she looked. He was, however, measuring against how old and clapped-out *he* felt. Richard insisted on helping with discarding the engine parts, and named them aloud as each went into the long skip.

'How did you get locked in?' she asked.

'Wrong turn,' he told her. She wasn't convinced, but didn't care to probe. He liked that. 'Sorry for your trouble,' he added belatedly.

She acknowledged with a self-conscious shrug. 'Cancer,' she said.

'Sorry,' he repeated. It *was* Virginia. Didn't she recognise him? If she did, she was concealing it expertly. 'Have you children?' he asked.

'A daughter. Do you have any?

'No.'

'Thanks for the help,' she said. 'What did you do to your shoulder?'

'I fell.'

'You're having a bad day?'

'As long as I can get out of here . . . .'

She smiled and he looked at her blankly. Life was mysterious. There were moments of daring and improbable symmetry, like this one in a rubbish tip. Richard wanted to embrace her, but his shoulder was throbbing, he stank of fish, and she was now anxious to move on.

'Virginia,' he shouted impulsively, as the station wagon pulled away. There was a flicker of response, but it might well have been nothing more than the guarded reflex to any human call. In any case, she didn't stop, and the car quickly disappeared behind a line of steel shipping containers.

Richard lumbered to this other security hut, where he explained his predicament.

'Sorry,' said the man in the hut, 'can't do anything for you. I don't lock *that* gate. I lock *this* gate.'

'I had to get something back,' Richard insisted.

'You didn't check in, did you?'

'No, I didn't check in. I was trying to catch up with the lorry.'

'You should have checked in at the gate.'

'You *must* have keys for both gates.'

'The tip-head is not my department,' the man said, with a sudden vagueness. It was clear he didn't like Richard. It may have had something to do with his impatience, and with the way he nursed his arm.

'Look, I've *got* to get out of here. Right now. You can open that other gate for me. *Please* open that gate.'

'Can't. Come back tomorrow.'

'There's nobody you can ring?'

'Nobody. And I'm closing up here in ten minutes.'

Richard raised the one hand he could raise, to indicate that the exchange was at an end. He walked out onto the road, looked left and right. Incredible, wasn't it, what life could dish out? He reminded himself of the steps that had led him to this place. That mental act seemed to bring on the rain. Flabby, acidic, lukewarm drops.

He looked for a taxi, but in vain. He decided to walk the long distance home. Then he decided to jog. He raised his face to the splattering rain, then lowered it again, made chicken's wings of his arms and began his jogging. Carefully, at first, on the broken concrete pavement, then more recklessly. He was still strong. Still healthy. He could accomplish this task. He found his rhythm.

He thought about Virginia. Decided that the woman he had just met at the dump wasn't Virginia Coates. Nonetheless, this resolute and winsome widow had provided a valuable service. She had made him think again about his mortality.

Richard wanted to say to Gloria that when he was dead there would be no ghost, no spiritual connection. No part of him would be lurking behind the hedge at their favourite park bench, nor floating in the ether as she walked their favourite cliff-top walk, nor sitting beside her in bed watching their favourite film, nor hovering by their favourite table at any restaurant they frequented. He'd be gone. He'd be nowhere.

But he also wanted to say there was a lot that could be done with not yet being extinct. They should give and take, and without delay.

A thousand yards on, he had to stop at a red light. Heavy goods vehicles and fast saloon models driven by short-tempered commuters flew by at dangerous proximity. Already he was tired and lopsided. Jogging on the spot, Richard used the time to work through the logistics of retrieving his car and the chair early the following morning.

He thought about getting home. Thought he might find Gloria sitting on their bed. He would say a simple hello. He speculated that Gloria might respond in kind. Who knew what might happen next?

The lights changed to green, but Richard didn't notice. He didn't see that the traffic had squealed to a halt. He continued to jog on the spot. When he got home he would take something for the pain. He would have a shower and think about the real Virginia Coates. He'd offer Gloria no explanation for the armchair. He'd talk to her about not being dead.

Gloria would be back in the apartment now, he was thinking. She'd have noticed that the chair was missing. His absence would be like his vanishing in a department store or in the aisles of a supermarket, but the chair – that would perplex her. She'd be staring at the empty space. He'd be staring into that space, too, when he talked to her in the bedroom;

when he was telling her that he was feeling better; when he was asking her if there was any hot water for a shower. He'd have to think of something to ask about her time out. Something good and righteous, and generous in spirit, before he told her about the city dump, his car, the chair. Say nothing about jumping into the dumpster, he was thinking.

As he jogged fearlessly over a stretch of crumbling pavement, Richard gave the impression of a man who had not suffered in life. It was every man's duty, he felt, to let the small, personal triumphs over adversity and heartbreak go unmarked. And now, at this stage in his life, he wondered what had been gained, what was his reward?

Already, the anxiety of his experience at the dump was falling away. This reserved man, who had an aversion to raw disorder, was having a second surge of recklessness, this one more glorious than the last. The meticulous nature of his work as an engineer bred sensible caution, but the less he worked the more cautious he became, the more he feared for himself. He was weary of the self-imposed limits and the tightness that came with his fretting. That tightness, he believed, had created his heart condition. It was time to let go. Time for a bull-charge.

He hadn't brought his little green leather pouch containing his nitroglycerin heart spray. He carried the spray in a pouch because he didn't want anybody to see what he had. Fat lot of use it was now, sitting at home on the kitchen counter. Pacing himself could be a matter of life and death. Good. He picked up the pace. He needed to be brave again, and he *was* being brave. Richard Meadows was alive and kicking. Wasn't that skyline something special?

2

The only people he saw were the huddled figures in cars, vans and heavy lorries hurtling by. There was nobody else, that is, until he saw the station wagon up ahead. It was pulled in at the curb, engine running, beads of moisture dripping from the exhaust. The silhouette of her head and shoulders at the wheel was fixed: it might have been a cardboard flat, but then he saw the light in her eyes in the rear-view mirror.

He stopped his running by the car. For a brief moment he clung with one hand to the heavy-duty chicken-wire fence to regain his breath. Then he stepped to the front passenger window, which she had lowered. He didn't lean in, but crouched to bring his face level with hers. He placed one hand in the door-frame. It was the friendly thing to do.

'I know who you are,' she said. Not 'I remember now' or 'Of course, I know who you are'. It was a straight admission.

'You do,' Richard assured her.

She made no comment about him being soaked to the skin. 'Get in,' she said. The light in her eyes was for him. The moment it hit the back of his retina he feared it would quickly fade, but he did not look away. His awkwardness drained from him in a shiver. He got in. They were old friends. It had just been confirmed. The car interior was warm from the blow-heater, and sweet-smelling.

The radio track was lit, but the volume was set to zero. She had turned it to zero when he had appeared as a small, jerky runner in her rear-view mirror. It was easy, this unexpected thrill, but then Richard felt there might be a stall. 'You were waiting for me?' he asked unnecessarily.

'I saw they wouldn't let you out with your car.' She put her hand on his thigh, leaned across and kissed him on the cheek. 'Will you come with me?'

'Yes,' he replied without hesitation.

Evidently it was easy for her too. The encounter at the dump presented itself as an extraordinary opportunity. That's what had them both limber. Richard had recovered his breath, and now his breathing became dangerously shallow. Her face broke with a lush smile. She gave out with a mock swoon. The sweetheart ease would hold for the short time that it was needed. The promise of serious sex tinged with sadness was irresistible.

Virginia turned up the radio before she engaged the engine. There was some dreadful talk show in mid-broadcast. That only made it cozier. The grumpy dump-man passed on his bicycle. He had pedalled hard from the dump-gates and now freewheeled past at speed, tyres hissing on the surface water. He had a filthy scowl for Virginia, who was parked illegally and caused him to veer.

'There's that dump cop bastard,' Richard observed without fear of breaking the mood.

'You have to come far to get your car back in the morning?'

'I'm a fool.'

'Richard Meadows,' Virginia announced contentedly, and pulled out into the main stream.

'That's me,' he said, resting an elbow in the window-frame. His reply managed to sound both weary and incredulous. Why should he know what he was doing? It was his subconscious mind that knew how he moved his muscles, not his thinking brain. His subconscious that first sent the message up the dumb waiter: time to take the nitroglycerin. This automation extended now to the sexual pull that had him trample any rationale for resisting. He was thinking he might have run his way to a heart attack, but now might ride his way to the same. This thrill might endure if he treated Virginia's intervention as a gift from the gods.

The rain shower had ceased. Virginia took a sharp left down a narrow side road. 'This way is quickest.'

'I don't know it, but then, I don't know where we're going.' He experienced a little wash of adrenalin down the rib-cage.

She looked over at him. Kept staring. It made the car go faster. 'You like to run?' she asked.

'Not particularly.'

The bonnet of the station wagon rose a little, then plunged smoothly into a great dip in the road.

'Virginia!' Richard shouted in alarm, but it was already too late. The car struck the dump-man, sending his bicycle sideways and under the tyres. The station wagon rode over his body with front and rear left wheels. There were no cries, just the rip of metal on the road surface and the flat, liquid sound of the torso being punctured by parts of the mangled bike. There was the dull thud of the tyres finding the road again, and the scorching brakes.

For a moment it was as though nothing had happened except that the car had come to an emergency stop in a part of town that quite naturally smelt of burning rubber. There was the sound of the fast-moving evening traffic back on the main road; there was soft breeze blowing through the nettles and tall ditch grass; there was Virginia's engine. Nothing else. Nobody else was about. There was just the dark lump on the wet road.

What happened next marked the beginning of a new and extraordinary intimacy in Richard Meadows' life. Virginia told him to wait in the car. She got out and went to look. She returned quickly to confirm that the dump-man was dead.

Richard got out of the car in spite of her protest. He went to see for himself. He circled the body, crouched beside it, reached out to touch the man's head with the fingertips of one hand, but stopped when Virginia said 'Don't'. How strange that the absence of life presented so clearly in the eyes.

Virginia was standing sideways, facing into the car. The exhaust pipe was dripping again. There was no movement outside the factories, which were set well back from the rusting fences and overgrown verges. She was looking left and right, up and down the road. There was light in the sky, but at ground level it was dropping steadily. She was watching for the glow of headlights beyond the rise on either side of the dip. This was a quite city laced with ribbons of traffic noise. She was listening for the sound of an engine peeling from the body of traffic a thousand yards behind.

'Richard,' she called from the car, 'will you come with me?' It was the second time she had said that. She was in shock, but utterly composed.

Richard got back in the car. 'Nobody has seen this. Look . . . ' she said with an uncanny mildness, 'we've only just met. You can – '

'No we haven't,' Richard interrupted, surprised and a little insulted.

'If you want to go to the police – '

'Do *you*?' He couldn't believe he had just uttered those words.

'Nothing would be made better. Only worse. We can drive away now.'

He threw open the front passenger door again. 'I'm going back. I need to make sure.' He got out and went to the body, looked again into the bulging, lifeless eyes. He put two fingers to the man's neck, but it was futile. Only now was he seized with the urgent need to get away. He sprinted the few yards to the car, fell in heavily, slammed the door. 'Drive,' he heard himself say in a short breath.

She said nothing. She put her eyes to the road and pulled away, driving slowly at first, then as fast as she dared as they ascended the incline. The body of the dump-man rose to the roof in the rear window before the crown of the hill wiped it from view.

'I can drop you somewhere,' she said. It was her first show of weakness – and triggered the first flush of panic in Richard. 'It will be as if we hadn't met – again.'

'I'll come with you. We can talk.'

'I'm responsible.'

'Dear God. You're sure he's dead?'

'Yes.'

'He's dead. I know he's dead.'

Neither of them said anything more for a time. They looked to the river of light up ahead that crossed east-west. Virginia, it seemed, wasn't engaged in the act of driving, but had arranged for the station wagon to be pulled through this expanse of industrial parkland on a steel wire, while she weighed what she had done, what they were doing now. She wrestled back control when there was the glow of oncoming headlights. She switched from dipped headlights to full beam and picked up speed. She kept the lights on full until a white van clouted past. They reached the junction with this second main artery about the time the white van skidded to a halt in the hollow just short of the lump on the road.

3

Richard was thinking he could go to the police. It wasn't too late. The police would understand that his delay was the result of shock. After all, it wasn't him who had run down the dump-man.

Virgina was holding fast. She would not be deflected. She wasn't thinking about policemen, or the rough-and-ready dead. Sorry. It was a tragic accident. The result of great bad fortune. Bad fortune could not be undone. It was her experience that it fell behind by the yard. She had killed somebody with her car and had run. That required glue-talk.

Their talk was a safety-valve interview. No, it was more like the soft opening to an interrogation that would end in sex. In all the world, neither of them had really decided what they should do, separately or together. Not yet. They were seeing how it felt to get away with it – just for now. They were testing their badness and their resolve.

'What are you, Richard?' The question was confusing. It seemed wildly out of order.

'What are you saying?'

'What do you do?'

'I'm an engineer. And you?'

'Painter.'

'A painter. You're a painter.' The reply was nothing more than an echo.

'I married. That changed everything. But now I'm going back to painting.'

'Your daughter…she's grown up?' he asked.

'Yes. She lives in Canada.'

'What's her name?'

'Clarissa.'

'That's nice.'

The traffic was moving steadily. *They* were moving steadily.

'You have children?'

'No. Your husband: when did he die?'

'Two months ago.'

'I'm so sorry.'

'Yes. And when did you marry?'

'Fifteen years ago. Thereabouts.'

'It's good?'

'Oh yes.'

'You can tell me her name.'

'Gloria.'

Oncoming headlights were beginning to bother Virginia. Richard chose to look out of his open window at the night sky, where stars were punching through.

'You know Gloria from a long time back?'

'Yes. A long time. Before college. We didn't get hitched for years, then . . . .'

'Where does the time go?'

'Yes. Where?'

'I'm glad we've met again.'

Richard shook his heavy head. 'I just can't believe what's happened.'

'No.'

Richard shut his eyes tightly, but they soon opened of their own accord. She was waiting for some improvement, and was now rewarded. Her bare response was so reasonable in tone, so deep and so measured, it made him plunge his hands between his legs. His lips parted, but whatever he was about to say didn't come out.

29

There was just the faintest flicker in her eyes. She snapped down the indicator and pulled out from behind a laden car transporter. He wanted to ask what it was she painted, but his question was choked in a cloud of diesel fumes.

4

His clothes were drying. They had him stuck to the seat. The wet had penetrated his bones. He tried not to shiver. He looked for distraction. Any distraction. They had come to a stretch of granite wall with a heavy overhang of dark green vegetation. There was a dense plumes of tiny leaves, which Richard thought might soon bear chocolate-scented yellow flower clusters. He tried to think of the name for it. Virginia slowed and flicked down the indicator wand, though there was no other traffic in sight. Under the circumstances this normal and deliberate act seemed excessive.

A the end of the wall Virginia turned sharply off the country lane and up a narrow gravel drive that snaked in a verdant channel. Richard struggled to remember the name of the bush with the chocolate-scented flowers. It was terribly important.

He needed to retrieve the name of this species – not as a distraction, but to demonstrate that all was right in his head. But the name wouldn't come.

At the top of the drive Virginia swung the station wagon into a double garage that was empty save for some tea chests and a pile of packing blankets. When they got out Virgina didn't look for damage to the car. Nor did she shut the garage door behind her. She just pulled a handbag from under the driver's seat, slung it over one shoulder and marched to the hall door. Richard's progress was altogether more hesitant. He stumbled out of the station wagon and lingered a moment, grateful for the stream of fresh, damp air he took into his lungs. He listened for sounds of the city, but there were none. There was just a breeze that ebbed and surged in the leaves above his head.

The house was nothing like what he had expected. It had a long, narrow leafy drive that wound its way in a deep track through a steep meadow. There were trees in the grassy banks on both sides, which made it impossible for two cars to pass each other. Richard had expected that she would take him to a nice three-bed suburban house in somewhere like Goatstown, but this was something altogether more impressive. A six-light dormer window between two tall chimneystacks, large bay windows fronting reception and bed-rooms alike under red-brick gables, small terracotta roof tiles that kicked out at a more shallow pitch for the last six ranks. A thick twist of creeper that was the wrong side of overgrown partially concealed a bright yellow door set in a shallow hall porch. Virginia waited for him with the key stuck in the door. When she turned the key and pushed, she let out a wedge of stale air that was laced with jasmine.

'Come in,' she said in a way that made Richard want to reach out and put his hands on her hips. She stopped in the doorway and turned to signal that this was truly the moment of decision. 'You *are* coming?' she asked with a sudden and piercing glare. She wasn't going to wait long for an answer. Should he cartwheel through the architrave? Or should he turn and resume his run?

He reached for his heart spray. Searched one pocket, then another.

'What now?' she demanded, diverting her stare.

'Nothing. I've forgotten something, that's all.'

33

'You've lost something? Dropped something?'

'No. I'll explain,' he said, pushing on through into the hall. He put his hand on his heart without realising what he was doing. She followed quickly, and swung the door shut and put her back against it. His impulse to reach out came again, but she beat him to it. She sprang off the door and threw herself against him.

'I'm so tired,' she said. 'Aren't you?' she asked, injecting a quick note of suspicion.

He couldn't help shivering. It was the damp in his bones. She must see that. His feet weren't about to surrender, but the rest of him was properly damned. If she had not already been pressed against him he would have fallen on her, whichever way his feet were pointing. She was an intent listener with soft, steady eyes. Her kind made things happen.

'Sit down,' she said.

He sat so quickly he nearly made her tumble. She poured two whiskeys without asking. Ice, but no mixer. In a few short moves they would be in bed together. It was the thing to do. Forceful coupling had its own cockeyed logic. Perhaps then, they might be in a better state to address what had just happened; what she . . . no, what *they* had done.

When he thought they had finished in her bed he felt wholly complicit. That, too, had its own logic.

'Aren't you going home?' she asked.

'No,' he replied. She found the steadiness in his voice deeply reassuring. There was a lot she had been about to launch into that she now let slip away.

'Not yet?' she added.

'Not yet,' he confirmed. 'We need to talk.'

Well, no they didn't. There was no talk of the accident, their behaviour in the immediate aftermath, their driving away in the night. What Virginia *did* say when she took both his hands and squeezed them tightly was: 'We can only help ourselves in this.'

It turned out these words weren't needed, either.

Richard went for a shower. Spent some time looking out through the bathroom window at the bright, early morning sky. He and Gloria didn't have a window in their bathroom. This was the perfect little window if you wanted to let your mind drift. There were columns of cloud on the horizon. Pink, creamy yellow, powder purple.

Later, standing at Virginia's tall kitchen window, the lighted cigarette she had given him fell to the tiles from between his fingers. 'Look at that,' he said, 'I'm perfectly relaxed.' And so he was. He bent down, picked the cigarette up, put it between his lips without drawing on it. He hadn't smoked a cigarette for twenty years. He had long harboured a desire to impersonate others, but any shivery stab at this showed Richard he had neither the nerve nor the skill. It was bizarre to be thinking about the business of impersonation in these circumstances.

Virginia urged him to go home, but he would not. She looked at him with her head tilted quizzically. It occurred to Richard that together they might indeed step out of this corner of hell. He had no experience of this kind of togetherness. And so, to bed again.

Richard woke in the late morning from a deep and luscious sleep, fully orientated as to what had happened the previous evening and into the night.

Richard Meadows: criminal. No nitro spray. No toothbrush.

The bed linen was stale, but the mattress was soft and there was that heavy jasmine smell again. Virginia was not in the bed with him. She was sitting at her dressing table with her back to him: it was an old-fashioned affair with wing mirrors on hinges, located in the dormer window. She was tugging hard on her matted auburn hair, working herself into a fury.

'Virginia,' he croaked plaintively.

She cursed. Her pin brush was in a hopeless tangle. With every tug she made the tangle worse. 'Wait,' she growled. Was she talking to herself? Richard didn't know.

'Stop,' he called. 'I can help.' Her impatience didn't fit with the steely resolve she had shown, and it unsettled him. He had made a terrible mistake.

'You'll want to get home,' she said, using the mirror to connect. 'Back to your wife.' She glanced at his pile of crumpled clothes on the chair.

He was already up and at the dressing table. She appeared older in this early morning light – more her age – but so did he. 'Let me see,' he said, staying her brush hand and examining the tangle. She was angry, but she let him have his way for now.

'You need to go,' she cautioned, but she didn't mean it.

'When we're ready.' It was clear there would be no talking through what had occurred on the road, or in her bed. Wise, he thought. He was willing to talk, but *she* had it right.

'Do you have pliers?'

Yes. There was a well-stocked toolbox at the back of the garage.

'Leave that as it is,' he told her. 'Come down to the kitchen. Is there coffee?'

He went to the garage, she to the kitchen. He examined the car for blood, bone marrow, brain matter. There was a small dent and some scuffing to the paintwork. The dump-man had gone under the tyres. There was blood in the tyre-tread. He got the garden hose, which was attached to a tap mounted on the wall, and blasted the crevices of the tyre until he thought he had washed the blood away. Then he found the toolbox and fished out a pair of pliers.

'What kept you?' she asked.

The smell of coffee made him slacken. 'I was listening to the birds.'

She slapped across the floor in ancient slippers, hairbrush hanging out of her head. She heedlessly poured coffee. He got her to sit on a stool, then set about extracting a cluster of brush pins from their cushioned bed. She seemed not to notice, or care.

'Engineer, you say,' she muttered. He didn't answer.

'There,' he said presently. She looked at the neat line of brush pins he had put in front of her.

'Thank you,' she said. 'Now go.'

But he did not go. Not straight away. He wanted to signal something; he didn't know what. He put his hand between her legs and she stood up and pushed into him as she had done the night before. 'Get out,' she said softly.

'I've cleaned down the car,' he told her. Telling her was a mistake.

'You have? You can go home then, can't you?'

'Yes.'

'No, you can't. You have to get your car.'

'Yes. Of course.' For a time he had completely forgotten his car. 'I do. I will. I'll go there first.'

'I'll take you.'

'Are you sure?'

'Why wouldn't I? You want to give me a number?' she asked on the way to the car. Now that he was about his business, she forced a slow pace. She deliberately held him back.

'Yes.' He wanted to give it. He didn't want to give it. He gave it. 'And yours?'

'I'll ring you. Then you'll have it.'

'Good.'

He got a bolt of fear, but it passed quickly.

5

Separate, but together, they drove to the city dump following the same route as before. No one travelled behind them on the link road. Richard half expected the impossible – a body still sprawled on the road – but there was nothing. There were no obvious scraps to indicate the scene of an accident, the location of the crime. No mangled bike by the side of the road. Did the police make chalk-marks? There were no chalk-marks. No rats. No carrion crows. Perhaps they hadn't killed him. Maybe he had crawled away.

When it came to the hollow, Virginia didn't stop. Nor did she slow down. Instead, she did something odd and dangerous. She swerved onto the wrong side of the road, so that the station wagon passed over the precise spot where the dump-man was struck. Richard shouted her name, but she failed to react.

He put both hands to his face. They rose out of the hollow in the certain knowledge that they would collide with anything travelling the opposite way.

But there was nothing between them and the far junction. She swung back to the left.

'I have a heart condition,' Richard bleated. It seemed a ludicrous thing to say.

'You do?' It made Virginia think of the sex they had had in her bed. She glanced across, her eyes glistening with excitement. Then she laughed, and he did too – which was bizarre.

'I need my spray.'

'Now?'

'Not now.'

She was so distracted that she misjudged the distance to the white line that marked the entrance to the main road. She made an emergency stop that flung them both against their seatbelts. Nobody in the passing vehicles showed any interest. The nearest pedestrian – the only pedestrian in sight – was five hundred yards away.

'It's best you get out here, love,' Virginia said. She leaned across and kissed him urgently.

He half fell out of the passenger door. 'Thank you,' he said.

'Thank you,' she replied. Then she peeled effortlessly into the nearside traffic and was gone. Richard turned in the other direction and stepped onto the kerb.

It was Saturday. There was no rush hour, but the sound of weekend traffic filled his ears. His body gave an involuntary shudder. It was cold in spite of the light. Unseasonally cold. He began to tramp the crumbling path by the chicken-wire fence. He saw the gates of the dump in the distance, and broke into a run.

There were birdwatchers who went to dumps. Gull-watchers, really. They would all know his dump-man, Richard was thinking. Would be used to giving him a wave. He could see one now on a ridge of high ground above where he had temporarily dumped Gloria's chair.

The dump looked the same to Richard, but of course it wasn't the same. How could it be? And there was a new man behind the glass. He gave

Richard a nod. Seemed like a nice chap. Looked eastern European. Polish maybe, or Latvian. Probably knew nothing of his predecessor. Dumping was going on as usual. Foreigner on the gate. It was a relief.

He was half expecting that when he walked through the gates, men would gather around him – policemen in plain clothes with bags under their eyes: *Excuse me, sir . . . . Yes, you . . . . Just a minute, please.*

But there were no police, just people dumping junk. Richard nodded to the new man in the kiosk, spoke through the glass in half mime: 'Left my car. Had a bit of trouble. Collecting it now.'

He was waved through, border-guard fashion. Richard nearly tripped over his own feet, but recovered quickly and shambled on. His car appeared smaller and shabbier than it should be. He didn't recall parking at such an awkward angle. He unlocked it with the key still in his pocket. The device gave a sickly little chirp. Locking the doors had been pointless, of course, as the boot was open. He stood in front of the boot and put a hand on the protruding leg of the chair as though it were a religious act.

Gloria's chair, too, seemed diminished and more worn than the chair he had taken from the bedroom.

'Dear God,' he muttered as a general offering, then went to get his mobile phone, which he had left in the gully between the two front seats. Gloria had rung three times. There were two brief messages from her, both in a conciliatory tone: 'It's me. I'm wondering where you are.' 'Me again.'

On the third call she left no message. Richard resisted the urge to ring her immediately. He also resisted looking to the concrete troughs in the adjacent yard. He stuck the key in the ignition, turned over the engine and swung about. He drove out through the gates without any gesture to the new dump-cop.

He drove carefully, without looking down the service road. He concentrated on concentrating. He needed to get clear of the numbness, and quickly. He needed to get back to his pathetic worries, his manageable crisis. He could do that now and be grateful. For the journey home he would fix on his wife, work the short-circuitry, demonstrate to himself that he was a jealous husband in need of a good thumping.

★

He concocts a scenario. He summons Tom Pearse, his rival, his nemesis. He knows about Gloria's infatuation with Tom. Knows about his interest in her. He pictures Gloria in her beloved chair at the bedroom window early one morning, one of those days he is out on site. Already, this is fantasy. She sees Tom gazing up at their apartment block. She goes down to meet him, but he has vanished by the time she steps onto the street. That's what has Gloria sitting by the bedroom window these mornings. The next scene he concocts has her driving a country lane to Tom's house. It's a beautiful pile in County Wicklow, set above a long slow bend in the road. People like to look and admire as they pass in their cars. They like his house on the hill so much, Tom tells Gloria, that every other year it's the cause of an accident on that bend.

'I'm here,' she says simply when he opens the door to her. She's standing before him in the nude now. Gloria knows how to hold her nerve. Poor old Tom. He doesn't know what to do. The vision puts a sticky crease in his heart. He kisses her full on the lips with a kind of sucking action. The greeting produces in Gloria an instant, but weary, delight.

This is the Tom who was unable to get his hands out of his pockets when he, the gallant Richard, jumped a tennis net to seduce Gloria, who was at his side.

'I'm here,' the naked Gloria repeats in the hallway, 'to say how sorry I am about your wife.' She is, indeed, sorry.

Tom cants his thick head. To Gloria the gesture seems exaggerated. She thinks his ear might come to rest on his shoulder. She speaks again urgently, to stop that from happening. 'I saw you in the street . . . my street . . . .' Her voice trails off. She is at sea. She needs to sit down.

'Come in, come in,' says Tom, sweeping her towards the living room. He is perplexed. For a moment he cannot recall what he is at. 'How's Richard?'

In this fantasy, Richard has Tom speak his name with a hearty burr.

'Not gone yet.' Gloria gives a hysterical laugh, which she suppresses with a shake of her head.

Tom rejoins with a booming laugh of his own, but it comes a little late. 'It's good to see you, Gloria. Sorry we lost touch.'

She sits down heavily in the middle of his couch. The room is untidy, but he has a fire going. There's a bottle of wine open on a cluttered desk, and a dimple of red in the bottom of a solitary glass. He sees her taking in the sheaves of paper with columns of figures.

'Tax,' he says, plunging his hands into his pockets and blowing out his cheeks. 'A tax audit, actually. Getting everything in order for an audit, that is.'

'Business is good?' she asks. She wants to shake her head again, but holds fast.

'Drink?' he asks, being the rude bugger that he is. 'Of course you will.'

When he comes back with two glasses of Pomerol, he finds she has slipped out of the only item of clothing she was wearing: her shoes. 'I won't be staying,' she says. There's no stopping them, except for the fact that Tom is a slow one. Has there been a terrible row with Richard, he wants to know. Her upset seems to him to be of a general nature. If she needs to be comforted, he wants to take a long run at it.

'I've been meaning to invite you and Richard over.' Lying bollocks.

'Have you? I see. That's nice.'

'Is everything all right? I don't want to pry.'

'Oh, you know . . . .'

Well, no. He doesn't. She looks at her shoes. They are strange objects. Certainly, they seem unfamiliar. She tells Tom that Richard has turned atheist. 'You still believe in God?'

The question takes Tom by surprise. He can recall no instance of Gloria being overtly religious.

'I do,' he hears himself say.

'Good for you.'

'I pray, that is,' he adds.

'I'm not talking about church-going.'

'I know that.' Well, this is bizarre for Tom. 'I have my doubts, of course.' Now *he* looks at the shoes.

'Of course you do.'

This visit is a bad omen, Tom decides. He's getting superstitious in his old age. He hopes Gloria isn't going to ask him to pray with her. But how attractive she is, still. He has a warm surge. He wants to take hold of her again and this time kiss her without the sucking, and squeeze her flesh, but she seems to be signalling that something else is called for. So far as he can judge, the shoes on the floor aren't about seduction.

Richard stopped with the shoes. The torture fantasy had been a useful distraction, but now he was pulling off the street, descending into the car park under their apartment building. He was nearly home. He didn't remember making any driving decisions on his journey across the city. The time it took didn't register. What he did now see was that his wind-up watch had stopped.

He parked in the street at the front of their building. He wasn't intending to stay. He was going to take Gloria out: drive her to her favourite restaurant and make a clean break of everything. He ignored a salute from Billy, his elderly neighbour, who was going out for a geri-jog in his white knee-length socks and blue runners. Richard pretended he hadn't seen him.

Billy didn't mind. He was wary of interrupting a man's silence.

When Billy was gone, Richard got out, took the chair to the lift, sat down on it for the ascent. When the doors slid open, he rose slowly, turned around, and reversed out of the lift carrying the chair as though it were a precious gift.

'Gloria,' he called on the landing. He had never done that before. Was it a warning? Yes, it had to be that.

Gloria wasn't home. Everything was as it had been when he left. He called her name again, more softly now, as he brought the chair through to the bedroom. Guided by the four dimples in the carpet, he returned her chair to precisely its former position by the window. He stood for a moment and listened. He heard the fridge click on. He went to get his little green pouch, which he had left in the kitchen. On the scribble pad by the house phone, Richard wrote a brief note to his wife:

> Gloria, my love, we worry too much. We're all right.
> You'll see. I'm down below in the café.

It was the pen that was trembly, it seemed, not his hand, but the line of ink came out smoothly.

How did he manage that? 'There, you see,' he said aloud. He could hold his nerve. He could follow through. He could suppress any fizzling doubt.

Before signing his note, he crumpled it and put the paper ball in his pocket. He returned to the bedroom, used the spray in his mouth – though there had been no alarm coming up the dumb waiter. He looked down into the street at his car. Over by the café he observed an old man getting ready to climb onto a tall black bicycle. The old boy took an age to bend down and unlock the frame from the railings. He needed a rest once he had wrapped the chain around the crossbar. With one hand on the ancient saddle and the other clasping the handlebars, he looked around as though he were lost. What presented as patience Richard saw as grim determination. An assertion that he was still capable, still in this world. Evidently he would soon fail, but not today. A shaky old man on two wheels was a danger to himself and others but, like everybody else, he was taking his chances.

Richard went down again in the lift winding his wristwatch. He didn't go to the café across the street. Instead, he got in the car and drove all the way back to Virginia's house.

6

As he wound his way up the drive he felt there was a different air about the place, but couldn't say what it was. When he stopped on the gravel in front of the hall door he saw there was another car in the garage. A BMW sports model. No sign of the station wagon.

He rang the bell. No answer. Rang it again and pounded the knocker. No answer. He walked along the front of the house and looked through the windows of the living room. They hadn't gone into the living room the previous night. He knew only the kitchen, her en suite bathroom, and her bedroom. He saw now that the furniture in the living room was gathered in the centre of the floor and covered with opaque plastic sheeting. Paintings had been taken down and were stacked in ranks face-in against the walls.

He went around to the back of the house, disturbing a pair of grubby magpies that flew over his head and away. He peered into the dining room. It, too, had swathes of plastic sheeting, which covered a long hardwood table and eight dining room chairs. There were more paintings covered and stacked against the damask-covered walls. He had an urge to try the handles of the French windows that opened onto the back lawn. So he did. He pulled down the handle, but the doors were securely locked. He was about to work his way around to the garage to inspect the car when he caught sight of a shadow passing in the hallway. It was a male figure. He quickly went back the route he had come, but was met by a bullish man who had come out from the hall door and was standing between Richard and his car.

'What are you doing here?'

'Hello. I'm just looking for Virginia.'

'Virginia . . . .' He was square on, his body limbered for action.

'Virginia Coates.'

'I saw you looking in the windows.'

'I'm a friend.'

'Friend of Stephen's?'

'Stephen . . . .'

'You didn't know Stephen? What's your name?'

'Richard,' he blurted, then struggled to stop himself.

'Richard who?' The man moved aggressively towards him. Came very close with his face. Richard pushed him away, both hands to the chest. The man stumbled backwards and fell on the ground. Richard flung open his car door, threw himself in behind the wheel, started the engine. The red-faced malcontent remained as he was, sprawled on the ground, making no move.

'I've got your number,' he said as Richard drove away, sending a spray of pebbles over the reclining man's head.

Richard snaked down the drive at a moderate speed to offset his shock, taking in great gulps of air. As he approached the electric gates they began to close. He dropped his foot on the accelerator and passed through with inches to spare on either side. He swung wildly onto the country lane and took the less acute of two possible arcs. Fortunately, there was nothing coming either way. He slowed to a crawl, then pulled into a neighbour's gateway, put on the hand-brake and wound down his window. He slid both hands to the top of the steering wheel and rested his forehead on the backs of his hands. He fixed on the sound of the wind in the trees behind the thrum from under the bonnet, but that was broken by the engine growl of a low-slung, souped-up saloon car he could not yet see. The sound triggered a dry retch in his throat.

A boy racer roared past in a white flash, and was gone. Richard could hear the breeze filtering through leaves again. A sweet floral scent on the air helped him regulate his breathing. He began to laugh. It wasn't a good laugh. It put a stitch in his tabid heart.

He had scarcely reached the bottom of the hill, from where the low city skyline was visible, when his mobile phone rang.

'Richard . . . .'

'Virginia. Where are you?' The urgency in his voice was unnerving for both of them, but Virginia carried through. She offered no direct answer. She said she wanted to meet.

'I want you to come with me.' It was the same emphatic seduction she had used outside the dump.

'Where? Come where?'

'To my flat.'

'Where? I've just been to the house.'

'I know.'

'You know? Who the hell is that at your house, Virginia?'

Again, no adequate answer. 'I'll explain when I see you. I really want to see you, Richard.'

They arranged to meet on the seafront in Dun Laoghaire. She had cropped her hair. She had a severe French boy cut, but it suited her. On the seafront they embraced like real lovers in angry heat. 'You came back,' she said.

'Hell of a greeting I got. Who is he?'

'He shouldn't have been there. His name is John Miller. The relationship is over.'

'He doesn't seem to think so.'

'What is he?'

'John?'

'Yes, John. What does he do?'

'He's in business. Property. What does that matter?'

'Property . . . . He knows your husband?'

'He knew him, yes.

'Knew him. Sorry . . . .'

'We both . . . .' She didn't finish the sentence. 'You want his address? You want to know about him because you got into my bed?'

'No.'

'I don't know where *you* live,' she protested.

Richard told her where he and Gloria lived.

'It's nice there.'

He got into the station wagon with her. It was crammed with art materials and domestic goods: nothing fancy, just kitchen utensils, heavy cushions, bed covers, everyday clothes. He didn't know what he was doing. He would know only when he spoke it out.

'Look,' she continued, 'you have just pitched into my life – '

'I should pitch right out,' he interrupted. 'I'm here to say that.' He hardly had room to move in the seat. He was talking over rolls of canvas, rolls of linen, rolls of paper. His head was tilted forwards, forced that way because of a tightly rolled duvet that was wedged between the car ceiling and the head-rest. 'And to say: you don't have to worry – about me.'

'All right. Go. Go to your wife, if you have a wife.'

But he couldn't go. Not just yet. He felt compelled to hold Virginia again, to lie down with her and to rut hard and be sorry for what they had done. 'I have a wife.'

'Go now, Richard. Are you listening?'

No. He was studying her hair, not listening, and she was glad. She looked at her watch.

7

Virginia drove into the belly of the ferry, then they went up on deck before it left port. She leaned on the rail, looking towards land. He leaned back against the rail and looked at her. It was a short crossing to Holyhead, then a long drive to London, to Virginia's flat: her new studio, new bed, new life. This was to be a brief visit to deliver the jumble she had packed into the car. In London she'd get started on her painting again. She'd be away from all the things that had inhibited her. The house in Dublin would be kept in mothballs.

When she told Richard her plan, there was nothing about the killing of the cyclist. The clarity that came with the denial was shocking.

They were still on deck, the ferry slipping out between the two pier lighthouses, when Richard's phone rang. He saw that it was Gloria. He showed the little screen to Virginia with his wife's name on it. Had it been the dump-man ringing, she would have been no less resolute. He didn't answer, and it soon stopped. There was no subsequent message.

Was Richard leaving Gloria? If he was leaving her, it was good to fill every waking minute with this madness; make it all about taking concrete, fugitive action. He kept his phone out. Got on the internet. Found what he was looking for, scrolled through it with eyes squinting and teeth gritted.

'There,' he said, positioning the screen of his mobile phone so that she could read the contents of the webpage too. He swallowed hard on the bare facts. Virginia read the few lines in the *Irish Times*: cyclist knocked down and killed, driver failed to stop. It gave the location where they had done what they had done. The victim was named as forty-six-year-old Michael Tierney, survived by his wife and two sons. She looked at Richard, nodded once with a melancholic smile.

He saw that she felt a little sick. He wanted to reassure her. 'That's all,' he said. 'There won't be anything more.'

Again, Virginia nodded. He terminated the connection and dropped his phone into his jacket pocket. 'Are you ready?' she asked.

'Yes,' he replied instantly. Ready for what, he didn't know. Anything, he supposed. He swallowed Michael Tierney, husband and father of two, whole.

They went and had a drink in the bar. John Miller, she told him, was her husband's best friend, had nursed Stephen along with her, had fallen in love with her, but it was finished. Dear Angry John was her former lover. He was now safely in the past. You and I are not yet lovers, she seemed to be saying, with her usual patience and directness; not like she and John had been – or, for that matter, her and Stephen. *You and I are bound under different circumstances. Ours is a different kind of fucking.* Angry John was ringing, but his calls were going unanswered. Virginia had a new number. She had bought another phone since she had taken the last intolerable rant from him demanding to know who this Richard fellow was who had come to her house.

The vessel cut smoothly through the inshore waters towards the open sea, which was unusually calm.

★

Richard slept in the car with bed-covers coming down over his head. On the outskirts of Birmingham he woke with a jolt, said: 'Sorry-sorry.' It was raining heavily. There were great heavy drops pounding the station wagon, demanding that someone speak.

'Aren't you going to tell me about your work?' he blurted.

'Talking about it just confuses me. I'll show you. Show you,' she repeated.

He was trying not to look like a buffoon, attempting to show genuine interest. Her answer was not reassuring. He pretended he had not fully woken and, indeed, he went to sleep again a short time later. He didn't dream of anything. He woke again as Virginia pulled into the Northampton service station.

'You had a long sleep.'

'Did I snore?'

'Yes.'

'Want me to drive the rest of the way?'

'No.'

'Good. I don't think I'm up to it.'

They drank tea. She took his hand across the table. 'It will all work out,' she said, 'except in the end.'

'You think?'

She flopped her head back, pretended she was dead. He let out a laugh he didn't know was inside him, knocked over his tea.

They were delivered to London inside a great swirling rain-ball which rolled east, leaving them alert and hopeful as they travelled the washed streets to a terraced house in Clapham. It was the last domestic dwelling on Stephen Graham's books. He had kept it with the intention of renovating it for the family. Virginia had lived there when she was a student at St Martin's School of Art, she announced. The house was still divided into flats. Richard counted five doorbells, saw the name 'Coates' hand-printed on a slip of yellow card second from the bottom. Virginia let them in with a key she had on a Texaco ring.

The interior was as grand as any house of comparable size and era, with fixtures and structural decoration intact, but it was threadbare and fusty. Over the fustiness there was the smell of spicy food - and cats.

He followed her upstairs to the front first-floor room, which was Virginia's flat. It was more threadbare than the common area, but was spacious. The walls were dry, the air fresh and damp. That could be explained by the one large sash window, which was wedged open with an ancient lumpy ashtray with 'Watney's Red Barrel' stamped on it. There was an iron bedstead with a thick mattress in one corner, two hard chairs tipped upside down on a box couch, in another. Neat piles of art materials, clothes and tinned food along one wall. Taped above was a series of bold figurative paintings with jagged lines which had been scored into blocks of colour on the canvas with the hard end of a brush. Richard took these in.

'Stephen,' Virginia said.

'Ah, I see.' He didn't.

'Sketches, to work from.'

'Sketches,' he repeated. She was going to paint up her late husband. Nothing wrong with that. John Miller had probably seen these. There was an ancient upright easel with an impressive crank-handle positioned by the window. Richard's eyes fell on the easel. Virginia stepped in beside it. He saw that she was happy to be here, but he must have been scowling at her, because she pulled a face.

'The bathroom is on the landing,' she announced.

'Thank you.' It sent him shambling out the door, which swung to in his wake. He stood for a moment on the landing, gripping the banister. He listened to the soft babble of other lives behind doors thick with layers of old paint.

Did he hear Michael Tierney's wife and two sons wailing and sobbing for the death of their bad-tempered husband and father? It was to be expected. 'I'll get your stuff up from the car,' he said through Virginia's door, but there was no reply.

The last things to come out of the station wagon were a record player with two heavy box speakers, and a stack of LPs. Rock music from the seventies, mostly with some exotic stuff: a few classical box-sets – opera and orchestral. She wouldn't let him put anything anywhere except in a pile in the middle of the floor. She had a precise plan, and the plan would go according to plan. She made up a second bed for her daughter, Clarissa, who would be coming to visit. Young Clarissa was her champion supporter and inspiration.

'Are you hungry?'

Yes. He was hungry. They went to an Indian restaurant on Clapham High Street. All orange and gold, with starched white tablecloths and heavy cutlery. This was where Stephen and Virginia had had dinner on their first date. He was already a high-flier, already making money from high-risk investments. He knew she liked Indian food. She was telling Richard all of this while she was stroking the inside of his thigh with a bare foot.

There was so much not to talk about, Richard was thinking. Fucking was what they both needed, until such time as they could talk about what they had done.

They had ordered too much food. Wine instead of beer. It was no time at all till Richard was saying: 'Look, one of those bottles that doesn't pour.'

8

The early-morning sun streaming through the window was making the figures on the wall jump when Richard stood again by the pile in the middle of the room. For a time he watched Virginia sleeping. Then he cast his eyes over the goods they had brought. It really wasn't very much.

She was trying to re-create her art-school days, pick up where she thought she had left off, grow again from there. She was desperate to get back a life that could not be recovered. She had cut her hair short, to let it grow again into the length and style it had once been. She was deluded, and Richard saw he was a plug-in. In a weak moment he thought he might be able to change that, but Virginia was painting her dead husband, and, no doubt, there were portraits of lovers. In time, she would paint the dead dump-cop.

He noticed now that there was a landline telephone sitting on one of the hard chairs. He picked up the handset. The line was live. It occurred to him that if he wanted to contact Virginia later she could easily monitor and reject his calls on her new mobile, but if this old piece rang she'd answer. He returned the handset to its cradle, and noted the number printed on the centre of the dial, in the same handwriting as on the doorbell tag.

He moved to the window and looked out into a bright London morning. A white flash of sunlight from a car windscreen caught him in the side of the eye. The bolt electrified the ghostly thing that had been crawling around in his head mumbling incomprehensibly since the accident. That milky little creature now lit up with a castrato shriek, then shrivelled and quickly died. Richard had been operating in a state of shock, but was now at exit point. He had a bad feeling.

'Richard,' Virginia moaned with uncanny innocence, 'I feel very close to you right now. I feel safe.' He hadn't heard her get out of the bed. She was standing naked in the middle of the room, looking at him through the vacant easel.

'Virginia, I think you should go to the police.'
She didn't speak. She let her eyes wander. 'I can't
bear thinking about it,' he continued. 'We both left
him on the road. I'll go with you. It's the right
thing.'

'We should do the right thing?' The lightness in
her voice was unsettling.

'We should.' Their creature lunacy had run its
course, hadn't it?

'All right,' she said. It was an acknowledgement,
not a declaration of intent.

'I need some air,' he said tightly.

'Of course. You want me to come with you?'

'No. You stay. You've things to do here.'

'You could go across to the Common,' she said,
awkwardly pulling on her dress, without
underwear.

'Yes. I know where that is.'

'Then we can go shopping for clothes and
shaving gear. You need to shave.'

He did go to Clapham Common, where the sun
shone on him and the four winds blew and
strangers passed with a blessed indifference.

★

Mr and Mrs Meadows were childless. There was just Richard and Gloria. They hadn't been able. It was down to his sperm. The engineer hadn't been able to engineer a baby. It had been difficult for them. No matter, they had found their way to accepting the fact. They had been good to each other.

It was this goodness and mercy that rang true now as he sat on a park bench to contemplate his next action in the face of uncommon regret. In life Richard Meadows had stayed alert to opportunities and had, in his reluctant way, been brave. Nevertheless, he had failed to excel at his work. The diagnosis of his heart condition had locked him with fear – until the shower incident, when he had been inspired to act.

And look where that had taken him. Head clamped in his hands, he studied the universe between his feet, until a crisp-bag blew across the frame and caused a switch to be thrown in his head. He rang Gloria. He was prepared to tell her the truth – *a* truth – he was in crisis, had had a sexual encounter with a childhood flame. It was a moment of madness. He was so sorry for any hurt he had caused. He was seeking forgiveness and under-standing from the woman he loved, the woman he had married; for better and for worse it was still the Richard she knew, but wiser, more emotionally mature – and he had a plan.

But Gloria didn't answer her phone. There was a long tally of missed calls from her, and now, no response. Served him right, he thought, but where the hell was she?

It seemed to Richard that there was little between being afraid and not being afraid. At a certain point they were interchangeable. I'm afraid; I'm not afraid; I'm afraid of something else now. There was, of course, such a thing as bad timing. Of late, he'd hold his little spray canister in front of his face and turn it in his fingers and think that thought.

He walked to Clapham South Tube station. Got on a train with the intention of going to Heathrow, where he would buy a ticket on the next available flight to Dublin. He squashed some facts together in his head. Virginia was grieving. She was trying to get back what could never be retrieved. She was in denial about the terrible accident. The killing. Her killing. Their running away.

He had already reached a block. He left the channel open, and waited.

If the journey across the sea and down the motorways to London had been made in a shellshock haze, the return was fraught with acute sensations and had Richard jumpy and wide-eyed – which was better.

On the Tube an American family got divided by the train doors. Richard was standing in the doorwell. He was the first person to think to manually prise open the doors that had clamped the buggy the mother was pushing. The little boy from the buggy was already in the carriage and had begun a panic-dance. The father was on the platform with the couple's daughter, who was older than the boy. The doors partially opened, then attempted to close again. The mother was determined to get them all in. The father was for getting the family back on the platform. There was shouting over the pre-recorded instruction to stand clear. Richard let go and moved to calm the screaming boy as the doors again clamped the buggy, and the father took up the prising.

'Come out, come out,' cried the father.

'Get in,' cried the mother. 'We're going.'

Make your plans as you will – career plans, family, travels to Timbuktu, to a dingy flat in Clapham, or from Waterloo Station to South Kensington – but life was full of rogue incidents, some of which required radical action. They were more out than in. 'Out,' barked Richard, and propelled the agitated boy towards the mother, who was now trying to force an entry. 'Out is best,' Richard shouted as he pressed the boy down into the buggy and joined the father again in pulling apart of the doors, which finally opened wide. The family was reunited on the platform. Whacked senseless, they stared into the carriage interior at the bold Richard.

The doors closed properly. The train pulled out of the station. Richard looked about at his fellow passengers, who graciously made no eye contact – save one, an elderly black gent, who nodded his approval. For that Richard was hugely grateful. The acknowledgement of strangers – that would be his only salvation in this new life he was leading.

He was sweating profusely. His limbs had gone weak. The incident had revealed to him just how tightly wound he was. He needed to change at the Piccadilly Line, but got off at the wrong station. Cursing and stamping and feeling light-headed, he made his way back via a pedestrian tunnel. He thought he might have to throw himself against the concave tiles and slide to the ground, but was saved by a rush of cool air as he turned a corner and shambled down a flight of stairs.

Practising stillness on the Piccadilly Line train, he broke his trance to use his nitro-glycerin spray, though he knew he shouldn't, as the danger had passed.

★

Take-off was delayed. Pilot and co-pilot had been grounded in a thunderstorm at Munich Airport, but would be on board soon. Richard looked at his trusty watch, but it had stopped. He had forgotten to wind it. Not good for a man seeking salvation.

'Newspaper, sir?'

'No thanks.'

'Are you the rubbish man?' the little boy in the adjacent seat asked the air steward.

'Yes, I am,' he replied. 'That's one of my jobs.'

Richard wound his watch. He wouldn't let the boy claim their shared arm-rest. For the entire fight he kept his backbone straight, elbows extended, and feet planted firmly on the floor. He resisted at first, but eventually let his eyes drift up the brightly coloured map in the panel above that showed the British Isles and a bit of France, and their enormous aeroplane tracking like an atrophied bluebottle. The map changed to show the British Isles, all of Europe and a great hunk of Africa, with various cities marked as far south as Dar es Salaam. He'd only be in the air for fifty-five minutes. How far could they go wrong?

'A drink, sir?'

'Yes please.'

He was going back to Gloria on a full short-haul jet clutching his car keys in his pocket. Bringing her or not bringing her his ruinous story, he didn't know yet. Oh, and that job with a good and reputable engineering firm he'd been about to chase after: he'd definitely lie about his health to get the post. Good to discover he had no qualms about that. Getting the car out of the multi-storey in Dun Laoghaire was going to cost a fucking fortune – not to mention the taxi fare from the airport to Dun Laoghaire. Things were looking up.

The white wine in the plastic glass was lukewarm, but he was having a second. And maybe a third. It went down quickly with a straight back. Virginia was grieving, yes. She was grieving. Rome with Gloria. Enough in the bank to see them through to the new job. It would all work out, except in the end.

He was retracing his steps, just as he had done when bringing back the chair from the dump. Good man, Richard.

In an elevated walkway at Dublin Airport, he paused for a moment to look down at a hare loping stiffly across a grass verge. The hare appeared to stop to look at him with the kind of terror that needed to be acknowledged. Richard tilted his forehead against the cold glass. Then, the thing that resembled a miniature kangaroo was gone and Richard was again on his way.

9

Jumping in a bin and taking the chair to the dump, that was about their marriage, about his mid-life crisis, but he had got out of the bin and had brought the chair home again. He might well have been a new man, had it not been for the chance encounter with Virginia Coates. Being lost and lustful was one thing; the actual fucking, quite another. A phony and unnatural euphoria had temporarily taken hold of him, but now he saw the light. This was the nonsense he was rehearsing for the short ascent in the lift, but really, what he cared about was that Gloria was safe and well.

Gloria wasn't at home. Didn't answer her phone. The apartment stunned Richard with its stillness and its personal silence. He changed his clothes. He shaved so closely, so severely, he almost took a layer of skin off. Red-faced and burning, he went to the café across the street, where he made a list of friends and family to call with his enquiries.

He kept looking up at their apartment windows in the vain hope there would be a shadow figure, a movement, a window being cracked open. His gaze drifted up to the fourth floor. He should knock on Fidelma's door. She might know something. Richard liked Fidelma, but she drove him mad. He admired her fierceness and her independence, her blunt, unsentimental flirting. What a relief it would be if Fidelma was giving Gloria one of her lectures on family and profligacy. She was Gloria's friend, not his. She'd be looking out for her no matter what.

Before he went back upstairs to knock on Fidelma's door, he rang Virginia's mobile. There was no answer. He should have left it there, but he didn't, not least because his life was filling up with a damp muteness that came with unanswered calls. He rang the landline in the flat in Clapham. He pictured the machine ringing on the chair. It rang just twice before the receiver was lifted.

'Virginia?'

'No. Clarissa. Who's this?'

'A friend of your mother's.' Ravi Shankar was playing in the background. She had Virginia's LPs out.

'Who?'

'Richard,' he blurted once again. He felt he should engage. 'How is Canada?'

'Excuse me?'

'Canada . . . I was just asking . . . sorry.'

'Have we met?'

'No. Your mother, she mentioned . . . ' *How is Canada? Plug it, you fool.* 'She's not about, I take it.'

'She's not here, Richard.'

'Will she be home soon?'

'She's in Dublin. I'm not sure for how long. A few nights, I expect. Do I know you?'

'Are you a friend of my father's?'

Persistent, like her mother. 'Yes,' he lied. 'Thanks again. I'll give your mother a call in Dublin.'

'I'll tell her you rang.'

'Please do.'

'She has your number?'

'Yes.' He thought she might be about to ask for a surname, mindful girl that she was. 'Bye-bye.' He ended the call. Ravi Shankar played on for a short time in Richard's head. He heard the primordial sacred sound '*Aum*' that came before a prayer. He waited. No prayer. Nothing.

The gates to Virginia Coates' house were shut. He got out of his car to press the bell on the intercom, which was set into one pillar. No response. He tried again. No response. He reached back into the driver's seat, turned off the engine, took out the keys. The boundary wall was more negotiable than the gates. He climbed over the wall. The evening light was fading. He tripped several times on dead wood and briar tangles, but was soon free and on the winding driveway.

When he emerged at the front of the house he was greeted by the sight of Angry John's sports car, which somehow managed to squat angrily on the gravel.

The hall door was open. Richard went in. 'Hello,' he called – which was a daring and outrageous utterance, under the circumstances.

John came down the stairs slowly. 'You,' he chided. He seemed very much more jealous than before.

'Me,' Richard properly replied, as Virginia began her descent of the stairs after John. Richard felt the vibration between the couple. It was unmistakable. John would never end it. Only she could do that. And, she had, hadn't she? She had ditched him?

It stuck him that this pair had been together very much longer than the few months since the demise of Virginia's husband, the late Stephen Graham – our man's good friend.

Virginia got John to withdraw to the kitchen. She took Richard into the atrophied living room and closed the door. This bullish hothead was frightened: that much was clear to Richard. He had lost Virginia and it was making him ill with rage and self-pity. He didn't look well at all. Couldn't they open the windows in this house, Richard wanted to know. It needed more than the hall door left swinging. They were all gagging on the stale, lifeless air.

He had come to assure her that he would not go to the police by himself, would not go behind her back. He would go with her to confess, if she would go. He wanted her to go.

She saw that he had come for more.

'I didn't expect you.'

'I had to come.'

'Your wife . . . ?'

He wanted to say that that was something separate, like her and John being separate from her husband, Stephen. But he didn't speak it out.

'It's not good?'

'We'll see.'

'I'm sorry if I have complicated things.'

'We,' he corrected her.

She told him now that she couldn't sleep because of what she had done on the road.

'You're taking stock,' he observed bitterly.

'I am,' she replied, choosing to ignore the bitterness.

Richard pointed over his shoulder. 'You and him?'

'We're finishing off.'

'Ah.'

'I thought we had already, but . . . .'

'It's taking another go.'

'He doesn't see reason just yet, poor John.'

'Poor John.'

Virginia's affairs were normally sequential. The
brief one with Richard, the engineer, was an
exception. It had overlapped because of unforeseen
circumstances, and now it too was finished, as
suddenly as it had begun. He and Virginia would
hold fast to their shared secret, their little dip in the
road. The accident was a tragedy for them also.
They would hide their shameful flight behind their
lust and their longing, which was itself a secret.

'You should go now,' she said, with a shivery
tenderness which he didn't like.

'And you'll be going back to London just as
soon as you've finished here,' he said with a
matching quiver. 'That is, if we keep our mouths
shut.' He had grown impatient. He wanted to leave.
This was over. And what was he thinking? She
wasn't about to confess.

'I will,' she replied happily to his question. She
shook his hand – which was an extraordinary thing
to do. Then she ushered him to the hall door. There
was no cruelty or misery intended in this action.
Simply, they had reached a terminus. His turn-about.

She took his face in her hands and kissed him.
He took hold of her wrists and pressed his elbows

into her breasts for a moment, then pulled away from her. Her eyes were sparkling, her face flush with life. He saw that Virginia truly came alive for the moment of parting, the getting out, the ending of an affair. Richard was impressed. Inspired, you might say.

'Goodbye, then.'

'Goodbye,' she said without rancour, without hesitation. He wanted to fold back on her, but knew better. She followed him onto the gravel, where she smiled again, but this smile fell heavily from her face and, for a fleeting moment, Richard saw again the expression of sudden longing that had mesmerised him when they had met in the city dump.

He wanted to reach out again and be doubly damned. But he did not. He experienced a convulsive wringing of the gut.

10

It came to Richard as he walked down the drive that this parting expression was a look Virginia and Gloria shared. With a startling tumble of primary cogs in his head, he found that he had done what his wife had been aching to do: in his own clumsy way, he had burst out. She had been sitting in her chair by the window, imagining an alternative life, making her plan to bolt. She had thought about doing it. He had done it, and now was full of regret.

Richard was going home. The nods and twitches he gave out with as he descended the lane were a manifestation of his incredulity at his jumbled fate. For all his regret there was, undeniably, this new-found confidence. This unearned reprieve. He walked with a distended belly, as if the waistband of his trousers was several sizes too big and he needed to expand to keep them up. He did not deserve this freedom, he was sure, but here it was. Azara. *That* was the name given to the species of dark green bush that overhung Virginia's boundary wall. He was glad the information had finally come to him. He took it as a good omen.

He slowed to a saunter between the high hedges and lifted his eyes to the late evening sky. He wanted to contemplate ordinary, uneventful stuff that might have happened had he stayed at home, but his mind filled with the animal detail of the accident. The accident he and Virginia had turned into a crime. When he stopped thinking about the cyclist, he thought about his jumping into the dumpster. His bravery, he decided, outweighed his clumsiness.

The chain of events got quickly wrapped around his neck. He wouldn't have been with Virginia had he not melded the remains of two bars of soap. He wouldn't have met her had he not taken Gloria's chair to the dump. Had he got to the dump a little earlier he would not have had to climb into the second enclosure; would not have had the encounter. Had she said: *Ah yes, I remember you, Richard. How lovely to meet. Must go.* The rubbish man wouldn't be dead had he, Richard, not recognised Virginia. Had she not waited by the chicken-wire fence with her engine running. Had he not got into her car so readily, the rubbish man would not have reached the dip in the road ahead of Virginia's station wagon. Would this very day be at the dump scowling through his window at members of the public meekly presenting with their waste.

With a little dart of phony euphoria, Richard realised he was again rehearsing that other life he hadn't led. He was exhausted, and utterly dispossessed. His heart might give out. He should contemplate for a moment the prospect of not getting the nitro under his tongue quickly enough. He should start at what might be the end. From there he could go anywhere. There was a new and stupendous clarity in Richard's life. From now on he would revel in familiarity. The narrow-bore heart that had so retarded his passion would convulse with relief and he would be at liberty as never before.

The unaccountable wind movement in the Azaras would open the gates, he fancied, if Virginia had not already opened them. If she was already upstairs rutting with her ex-, ex-lover.

Funny how himself and Virginia didn't talk about their childhood, their early infatuation. No, it wasn't funny. Not one bit curious. He had to get home urgently to Gloria and see what life he might yet make with her.

It was fitting that he finish off his torturous little fantasy about Gloria visiting Tom, finish it firmly in his own favour and clear his mind of it. He projects back to the naked Gloria with her shoes on Tom's rug in front of his couch. Tom looks up from the shoes, rips his hands from his pockets, pulls Gloria off the couch and kisses her awkwardly. He's not going to stop, is he? He's going to thank the gods for this good fortune and take Gloria to bed immediately. But this is Gloria, don't forget – naked or otherwise. She'll not be taken advantage of. Richard is the lucky one here. Gloria thanks Tom for his wine, the wine she has scarcely tasted. She indicates with a glance that she is about to leave. 'I only came to offer my sympathy,' she says.

'You came about Ella?'

'Yes. I did. I'm sorry you've lost her.'

Tom has difficulty getting his hands back into his pockets, but he perseveres.

'Have another glass with me,' old Tom says, dipping one shoulder. He's pathetic, and he knows it, but Gloria has no clothes on.

'Lovely to see you again, Tom,' she says, pushing him away expertly. She stamps into her shoes and goes to the pile of clothes she shed at his hall door.

Richard pictures himself in the shower when Gloria turns the key in the lock and enters the apartment. She comes into the bedroom. They greet each other with a civil familiarity. She sits at one end of the bed. She waits for him to dry himself and come out to her. She spreads her hand on the duvet, indicating that he should sit beside her. Which he does.

Richard finds it hard to halt the gushing fantasy. He needs a stopper. Gloria, he decides, arranges for a weekend trip for them to Rome. She pays for it on her card, then buys herself a new pair of shoes. The dumpsters are larger in Rome,

Richard notes, while he gazes out through the side-street plate-glass window of the department store where Gloria is choosing an expensive outfit he fully intends to pay for. It's on this weekend break in Rome that Richard speaks to Gloria about not being dead. She sits on the edge of her café chair and listens carefully before answering with a simple acknowledgment. There is something in the mélange of sound from the surrounding streets that robs their words of their weight, and soon they are crossing the piazza together inhaling the smell of flowers, burnt sugar and traffic fumes. This is a fantasy he can stand over. It can be converted.

There were no car headlights. Something stirred in the adjacent hedge, and a small dirty white shape scurried across his path, almost under his feet. As for John's car, he heard it approach only seconds before it struck him. It fired Richard along the lane in a corkscrew tumbling motion. He passed through a gossamer caul of flaming white stars. There was no air in his lungs. The impact had knocked it out of him, but he was not compelled to breathe. He should try to sustain this spin, the engineer thought, if the world was not to end. In the event, his movement was terminated by the narrow trunk of a mature larch.

It was the end of this thing that had begun with a bar of soap.

★

The police made no connection between the two fatal incidents. Their enquiries continued, but no significant information came to light. Gloria was unaware of a cyclist being knocked down and killed on a narrow service road near the city dump, let alone that there might be some connection with her late husband.

When Richard returned to a deserted apartment after that first night with Virginia, he was not to know that his wife was a few yards away with Fidelma on the fourth floor. She knew nothing about his trip to the dump, and nothing of what came out of it. Nothing about any romantic trip to Rome.

The autopsy did not support the theory that Richard had suffered a heart attack and had staggered into the path of an oncoming vehicle; nonetheless, this was what Gloria believed. She could not, however, explain how Richard had come to be on foot and wandering in the industrial wasteland where his body was found.

Fidelma proved herself as a true friend and unflinching supporter. Gloria's old flame, Tom, rang to offer his sympathy as soon as he heard the news. That was a comfort.

Part 2

John Miller

11

There was a property in Putney that had to be cleared of squatters. John parked his car two streets away. It was the wise thing to do. In the early days there had been an incident with a brick through his windscreen. People jumping up and down on the bonnet. He had done with much of that front-line stuff, but today there was nobody else available to do it. He went to Putney on that dark, wintry day to speak firmly but courteously, in a slack sort of way. These were hoary old hippies with suction pads on their feet. Patience and a timely bribe was the way forward, John was thinking, but he had a date and was in a hurry. In the event, he offered the bribe on arrival. To begin with, they weren't having it, though they were set to go and there were packing boxes in the hall. They wanted the offer sweetened.

John's date was with an Italian. She was a student at the LSE. Just started. She was a nice, sophisticated girl, self-possessed and magnificently standoffish. What was he thinking? He should stand her up. The visit to the hippies, with their righteousness and their tea and the bit of hash-cake they'd given him, had thrown him.

The Italian didn't know London well. He had arranged to meet her outside the Odeon, Leicester Square. He upped the offer to the Putney brigade, got a result, sped into the West End, managed to get to the appointed spot on time. The whole of John's life ran on high octane in those days, but gratification, he had found to his dismay, was illusive.

The leaden sky opened and it began to pour. John slipped into the National Gallery via the Orange Street entrance and let his car-coat down from over his head. He wandered a while, the wet coat draped over his tightly folded arms, not thinking about the Italian girl, the hippies, or himself, for that matter. He couldn't settle on a route through the building. He must have looked lost. He was thinking he, might sit down, when a woman spoke to him. She was on her own. She walked over to him directly and struck a smile.

'I know your face,' she said. She didn't. Not really. She liked his face. Was drawn to it. She had seen him somewhere, it was true.

John went blank for an instant, but perhaps it didn't show, what with the hippie-shit. 'Hello.'

'Where have we met?'

'You have me there.'

'Not here. You're from Dublin?'

'Me. Yes. And you?'

'I know you from there. Or somewhere.' She moved closer.

He put out his hand to shake. 'John Miller.'

'Virginia Coates.'

'Virginia,' he echoed, as if her identity might fall into place.

'You're meeting somebody?'

'Well, yes. Not in here. Outside.'

'A date?'

He liked her impertinence. It seemed to be guileless. 'Yes. And you?' He liked this freshness, but couldn't think why he was so nervous. Perhaps he wasn't nervous at all. Shouldn't have taken the

Putney cake if he wanted to know fully what he was at.

'Yes, yes. Meeting a chap who should know better.'

'Ah . . . I see.' He didn't.

She told him she was attending St Martin's. One of her fellow students was coming to get a lecture from her. They'd been having a dispute. She wanted to get him thinking right about the human body. There were paintings she wanted to rub his nose on, then they were going next door to the portraits. 'Then, we're going to bed.'

She wasn't trying to shock him. Curiously, he could tell. Still, it was too much information, and he told her so.

'There's a lot to share,' she said. 'we'll have a full day – once he gets here.'

'Sounds lovely,' said John.

'You think?' She was glad John Miller approved, even if he showed signs of faltering. 'You want to walk with me?'

'Yes,' he heard himself say, 'but you'll want to meet you friend?' It was obvious yer man wasn't coming.

'He'll find me.'

'Look, it's all right if you don't want my company.'

'No, no. It's just I should check . . . .'

'For your friend outside?'

'Yes.' Now why was he doing this? Those gobshite hippies. But he couldn't blame them. Whatever hash-haze there had been had now lifted. There was no denying he was thinking straight.

'If she doesn't show, you can find me,' she said.

'Yes. I will indeed.' What a beautiful, warm smile she had. He looked about for his way back to Orange Street.

'Main entrance is that way.' Virginia pointed with her hip.

'Yes,' he said. 'Right.' And went as he had been directed. He took his time. Found it a pleasure to rack his brains about Virginia Coates. Where might he have seen her? London, most likely. *Or somewhere*: the way she had tossed that away. His progress to the main entrance was slow. He turned a corner and found Virginia sitting on a bench, staring intently into one corner of an Italian Renaissance landscape.

She was waiting for him. No doubt. The staring didn't fool John.

'Aha . . . .'

She was holding back on the figurative work, she told him, 'but to hell with fucking Charlie.'

Charlie was never going to pitch up. She must have known that.

'Come on,' she said, linking her arm through his. She was glad to fight the wet wool coat for space. 'You show me something.'

They wandered through the rooms like a well-established couple. Anyone taking a passing glance at them would think they were a settled couple who might well make love on the couch before they had their tea that evening.

Life was rich.

Look. Ah yes. This way. Can we just go in here? There was no lecturing from Virginia on the human form. The rain pounding on the galley roof made the pictures vibrate on the walls for the besotted John Miller. He looked at his watch just once.

'What time is it?' Virginia asked, quick as you like.

He angled his watch.

'You've dumped her. It's official.' She kissed him lightly on the cheek. 'Come with me.'

★

They stood a moment peering through the rain-smoke, at the square.

'She's not here, your date?'

'No.' Richard made a little performance of looking left and right at the huddles of people sheltering under the colonnade. 'Charlie?'

'No sign.'

They walked out into the rain. She pulled on a red woollen hat.

'You want to come under my coat?'

'No thanks, John.'

They were soaked to the pink by the time they got to the car park. Droplets fattening in their eyelashes. Rivulets streaming from the tips of their noses. They drove to her flat, a terrible little dive in Southwark. Something that was once a corner shop, then a store-house, now part store, part partitioned flat.

'Good God.'

'What's wrong with you? It's only temporary.'

They peeled off their sodden clothes. She put on

PHILIP DAVISON

'The Girl from Ipanema' on her record player. They
lay down under a reproduction of Caravaggio's
Doubting Thomas, with his finger in Christ's spear-
wound. The coupling was luscious for them both. Real
passion between strangers. Strangers' passion. Wasn't
it wonderful what life could randomly put your way?

There was a heavy knock on the door.

Charlie.

Charlie was not what John expected – not that
he was ever expecting to see Charlie. Tall, skinny,
sloping shoulders, lank hair which was plastered to
his head because of the wet, large brown eyes,
outsized mouth. 'Have you anything to say to me,'
Virginia?' There was something inappropriate
about his delivery. It signalled hurt and offence in a
lazy south London accent.

'If you're here on your high horse, I'm not
interested,' Virginia replied, with remarkable
patience.

'Where were you?' he asked slackly.

'With a friend in the gallery,' she answered, as if
John were invisible.

'*I* was in the gallery. I waited half the blood day
for you.' He couldn't seem to slip up a gear,

increase the temperature, tighten the skin around those eyes even a little.

'You didn't go looking, did you?'

'We said at the foot of the stairs.'

'You didn't look.'

'Of course I looked. You need a holiday, my love. Get your head right.'

'There'd be too much pressure to enjoy myself.'

'I'd go with you, only it wouldn't do me any good.' He put his nose to her breast. 'What's that smell? I haven't smelt that on you before. I prefer the old Virginia.'

Well this was bizarre. John was in a guerrilla play, standing stage left, waiting to make his presence felt. 'Excuse me . . . .'

'Are you fucking our friend here?' Charlie asked with the same flatness, except now he was pointing limply at John.

'Excuse me, pal . . . .'

'It's all right, John,' Virginia said.

'Yes, it's all right, John,' Charlie echoed, 'I'm well used to it. Is that your car outside, blocking the way?'

John Miller gave Charlie a drubbing, but not before Charlie gave him two black eyes. That, too, was unexpected. John didn't see the narrow, bony fists coming down from a great height.

Virginia intervened. She wrestled them both while they fought, then got Charlie out the door.

It was hard work, but Charlie held his bloody nose and put in the nearside headlight on Miller's car with the heel of his boot.

It was Charlie, you could say, who provided Virginia with the connection to Stephen Graham, and John who made the introduction. When Stephen saw John's black eyes, he wanted to meet the woman who had been the cause of the affray.

A week later, John moved Virginia out of the flat in Southwark and into a flat in a house in Clapham that Graham & Co. had just bought. Four months later Stephen and Virginia were engaged.

John, too, had fallen in love.

With Virginia.

Without her knowing. Knowing, and responding, would come later.

At St Martin's, Charlie went entirely abstract.

12

That was a long time ago, and now, Stephen and John were in London together to conclude some business. They were choking off an operation that was about to lose a lot of money. Smart remedial action: that was a feature of Stephen Graham's business practice. He had a reputation for being astute and clever with his solutions where others would panic. John was the quiet one at meetings. The capable persuader, one-to-one. The enforcer. It was Stephen who had tutored John in the business of imminent failure.

They were due to fly home, but Stephen suggested they stay in town and catch a later flight. He wanted them to go to the American Bar at the Savoy Hotel. 'I like it there,' he said, out of badness. John did, too – though he was more fastidious, and secretly feared that one day soon he might run out of privilege, just as a man might run out of sperm.

'I'm up for it.'

'You and me, John. You and me.'

'You want to get drunk?' John's eyes were burning with compassion for his pale, beleaguered friend.

'I haven't done anything foolish for a long time. I feel a bout coming on.'

'You want to make fools of us both.' John was seeking confirmation.

'In my case, it will pass.'

Was this the beginning of some final game-plan starting to play out? 'We can get drunk and talk sense. Talking sense will save us. That's always the hope.'

'Always hoping, John. Never go into business with your friend, right?'

'Right.'

'We've done well.'

'We have.'

'*You've* done well.'

'I'm not finished.'

'John, I'm afraid.'

'I know.'

'No harm being afraid, you'd say.'

'None.'

Before going to the Savoy, Stephen took them to a jewellers' in Knightsbridge. He wanted to get Virginia a present. Something special. He bought her a gold ring with a high-set emerald. He seemed to have it already picked out.

'I see how steady you are,' John said in the taxi to the hotel. 'How calm. I know what that is.'

'You do?' said Stephen.

'It's despair. You're an ill-content.'

Stephen could see that his friend was trying to humour him, trying to show a bit of robust humanity. 'I am.'

'I've been that: an ill-content.'

'In despair . . . ?'

'No. Never so steady. Thankfully, never quite so calm. That's a beautiful ring.'

'It is, isn't it?'

'Virginia will love it.'

'She will.'

When they had sat down in the American Bar and ordered their drinks, Stephen placed the smart little bag on the table and said: 'Here, John, I want you to give it to her.'

PHILIP DAVISON

'What?'

'I already have something for her. You give Virginia this.'

John felt sick in his stomach. 'Stephen, I don't follow . . . .'

'I know what you're doing. I know about you and Virginia.'

John performed a series of deep optical shifts, which ended with direct eye contact. Their drinks arrived promptly. Stephen thanked the waiter with a bidding smile that made for an express withdrawal. 'We're here – just you and me – to drink and talk about Virginia.'

'I want to talk.'

'Don't worry. I forgive you. I'm finished. I need somebody to look out for her and Clarissa. You're the man for me.' He took a mouthful from his whiskey glass.

'Stephen, I can't tell you how – '

'Have your drink.'

John took a generous gulp of his whiskey and soda.

'You're not like the others,' Stephen said. John nearly choked. 'There's nothing for you to worry

110

about. They're in the past. You've been up in her studio space, of course: the studio she can't work in?'

John nodded. Evidently, Stephen needed him to speak. 'Yes,' he admitted. 'I have.'

'She has me up there too, on occasion. I like it, don't you? I've told her we could rework it: the space, I mean. Create a different kind of studio. But she says no, it's fine the way it is. Counts herself lucky, she says.'

'Stephen . . . .'

'You get a fire going up in that room and it's really very comfortable. No one to bother you. Nice view to the east over the treetops.'

John was struggling. He had another mouthful of his drink.

'Nice little nest, don't you think, John?'

'Yes. Nice.'

Stephen drank from his glass and let out an appreciative sigh. 'Strange to say, she loves me. I know that much, and she doesn't doubt that I love her. *There's* something never to be taken for granted.'

There was a silence. The two men were sitting beside each other and, together now, they belatedly took in the familiar surroundings. There were only a few patrons. Lucky people, they seemed to both men.

'I captured Virginia,' Stephen said, leaning a little in John's direction, 'not the other way around. Time for me to let her go.' He laughed at his own bittersweet words. 'Fuck – I can say that *now*.' Let her build her world again around her painting. Let her get close again to Clarissa. Have you look out for them both. Are you listening?'

'Yes. Of course.'

'She needs to go forwards. Not stay stuck. She can be free.'

John nodded giddily. 'Of course,' he repeated. He turned his chair around so that he was facing his friend. So that he might squarely take all that was due.

'God, I love this place,' Stephen said. He downed the last of his whiskey smoothly, as though normality was about to burst through. 'Finish that. We'll have another.'

There was more drinking, but it was tempered. In the waiting lounge at Heathrow Airport, both men sat at a plate-glass window. John had his arms wrapped about the satchel he cradled on his lap. Stephen had thrown his briefcase under his chair. They looked out into the night sky.

'Sorry we missed the flight,' said John. 'My fault.' He saw that his friend was very tired.

Stephen's response was, nonetheless, steely and charged. 'Lateness . . . late arrival . . . showing up late . . . it's not the same as coming to it late. That kind of lateness is the product of slow thinking. The overcoming of confusion at a late hour.'

John was silent.

'Wouldn't you agree?' Stephen demanded.

John made no reply.

'Have you nothing else to say to me?'

'I'm thinking,' said John.

There had been no talk of betrayal. No apology sought. It didn't seem right. Not even appropriate. They would be keeping Virginia out of their reckoning, so far as they could. 'I understand why all this has happened,' Stephen said. 'I don't like myself for being so understanding.'

'I want you to know – '

Stephen cut across him: 'What kind of husband would I be if I didn't see the attraction, I hear you say.'

113

'No. I didn't say that.'

'Now, there's the question of your punishment.' This was more than an ironic barb. John needed to register his deep regret, but Stephen had indicated that the regret was to be taken for granted. 'I'm thinking about the future.'

'I see what you're doing.'

'Making provision . . . .'

'Yes.'

'Virginia is looking for a new life. Perhaps she's told you as much?'

John mumbled hesitantly.

Stephen continued. 'Don't believe it. She wants an anchor. She wants to go back, get what she thinks she's lost.'

'Most of us – '

Stephen cut in again: 'You nail her down. You get her to commit.'

'I will,' John said. 'I will,' he repeated.

'She won't thank you for it. It has its own reward.'

This was a terrible ordeal, with all its promise, but in truth, John cared more about loving Virginia than he did about his friend – which was expressly what his friend wanted. Nothing else mattered. 'I swear, I'll take care of her.'

They watched two jets climb into the air before either of them spoke again. Watched them until they had vanished. 'She chose you, John.'

'I love her.'

'I'm sure you do.' Stephen reached across and patted his friend on the knee. He got him to agree to sell his stake in their business at a knockdown price. Clarissa would benefit. 'You start something new. See how you fare.'

13

Virginia had not abandoned her husband, and would not have to do so. Stephen Graham was wise enough to know that his wife would throw over John Miller. That was the real punishment.

Virginia had chosen John and made it seem that he had chosen her. His blind love for her assumed that she would be willing to stay with him, which she was not.

There was no talk of betrayal. No expression of regret. Just the drive on both their parts to continue regardless. What else could they do?

Part 3

Gloria Meadows

14

Gloria was seeing her husband in familiar places. Being a court stenographer, her noting of these appearances was meticulous. She saw him on their street, in the café, by the park railings, passing at the far end of the fruit-and-veg aisle, but not carrying through into pork and dairy. These were skilfully choreographed, fleeting glimpses. He was not making ready to engage, but rather to rack her conscience. He was there and not there to haunt her, jingling change in his pocket and pretending not to see her. Being his usual solitary and uncommunicative self, demonstrating that nothing had changed, except that he was dead. One of the Lord's many refuseniks lost in His clover demesne. 'Close your eyes,' she heard the phantom Richard say, 'and I'll shut mine.'

'I do believe,' she had told the nervous young Richard, as they were walking out through the

college gates on their first proper date. The slight
echo in the entrance arch was suddenly more
pronounced. He thought she meant: believe in
them, as a couple. That was altogether premature,
not to say desperate.

'We have time for a drink,' he said out the side
of his mouth. 'I've booked the table for eight-thirty.'

With her quick, bright eyes, Gloria saw that the
hinge-nuts on his jaw had tightened, that she
needed to be specific. 'I'm talking about God.'

'Oh. Him.'

'That shocks you, I know, poor liberal wretch
that you are, Richard,' and she squeezed his hand.

'No, it doesn't,' he lied. 'Not one bit.' He headed
this piece of information over Trinity railings and
returned the hand-squeeze, but his squeeze wasn't
quite so convincing, and seemed mistimed. True, he
had seen the lovely Gloria through the chaplain's
window bouncing her bottom with laughter on a
hard chair. That was about sex, maybe. The
unattached chaplain was a handsome fellow and,
presumably, hard to get.

Gloria wished she had been there in the ditch to
stop Richard staggering onto the road, to gather

him up, to open his mouth and administer his heart-spray. She wished she had been there to lift his head onto her lap until it could rest on the flat pillow of the ambulance. To have got them to ring merry hell out of their siren. To have not let them cover his face. To have done that.

The police weren't satisfied that Richard Meadows had been killed at the location he was found. They didn't believe he was struck by a vehicle and propelled into the ditch, nor did they believe he was hit and staggered or crawled to the ditch. They would proceed on the basis that the incident had occurred somewhere else. They had not yet completely ruled out the possibility that Mr Meadows had been pushed from a height – a premeditated act, or manslaughter – followed by a panic dumping. The damage to his body was consistent with such trauma, but forensics suggested otherwise.

So, where was Mr Meadows slammed? Who had done it, and why? Detective Barrett was in charge of the investigation. It was shaping up to be his first murder case. When Richard Meadows was slid into the refrigeration unit, Detective Garda

Barrett stood looking into the ditch, considering the physical evidence and contemplating deviousness and heartbreak. He wasn't feeling the best, but was determined to see out his day, then get to bed early. He could think in his bed if his guts allowed.

15

Detective Barrett went to see Gloria first thing the following morning. He had talked with her several times, but this was his first house visit. He stepped in sheepishly from the hall and moved across the living room to the walnut upright piano. 'Do you play?' he asked softly. His eyes were narrower and brighter than before.

'It sits there, mostly. It was my father's.'

Barrett was a methodical man who taunted himself with capricious flights of flim-flam. He was a cautious but steady mover who vacillated in his desire to leap forwards. He liked his pleasures – such as they were – organised. He could not help his self-conscious demeanour, which was easily mistaken for reticence. There were colleagues who were surprised and irked by his recent promotion, and who quietly predicted an early fall. 'But you play?' he asked.

'I play badly.'

'Do you mind?' he continued, drawing up in front of it and indicating with an open hand.

'Go ahead.'

He lifted the keyboard lid, formally composed himself, and played a brief passage from Satie's Gymnopédies, which he did with light fingers. The policeman can play, Gloria thought, but his timing is off. He plays with nobody listening.

'Lovely tone,' he declared. 'Needs tuning, of course, but you know that.'

'Yes.'

'Thank you,' he said, lowering the lid. He brushed the walnut surface appreciatively. 'I'm sure you don't play badly, Mrs Meadows.'

Barrett broke from his piano excursion by pushing the stool under the keyboard as far as it would go. It was time to return to the order of business. It was no surprise to Gloria that he came at her again with a recap. They would talk through what had happened, making a deliberate reduction, asking questions again...

'Your husband went missing on the Friday evening?'

'Yes.'

'After – '

'Yes. After,' she said emphatically. She had told Barrett of their row, though it wasn't a row as such.

'Had he gone missing before?'

'We've had our rows, of course, but he never – '

'Went missing.' They were both nervous. The repetition had done nothing to reduce their anxiety about their duty to the dead Richard.

'You tried calling?'

'Yes,' she answered, 'I tried.'

'Six or seven times.'

'Something of that order.'

'And he – ?'

Didn't answer.

'He rang you later?'

'Yes.'

'But *you* didn't answer?'

'No.'

The detective made a brief pause, then said: 'I understand.'

Gloria looked away to the window. 'He must have been in trouble – '

'We don't yet know the sequence of events.'

'But I didn't answer.'

'It will be easier to bear when we know what exactly occurred.'

'Yes.' She wanted to believe him, but was convinced he had no idea how he would establish what had happened. He might be holding back important information, Gloria privately conceded – holding it until he had a fuller picture. There may have been sightings. She herself could conjure no reliable image of her husband at large in that landscape. She simply couldn't imagine what he had done, or where he had gone, or how he had come to be wandering across wasteland on the edge of the city. He had become disorientated, perhaps, had got hopelessly lost, but that was so unlike him.

'Mrs Meadows . . . .' Barrett was calling in her attention.

'Yes. What is it we can do to find him? I mean, find where he has been?'

'Can we go through it again: his leaving the apartment?'

'Yes. Friday evening . . . .'

When Detective Barrett moved to the study, Gloria stood resolutely in front of the mirror. I look like a widow, she thought. I look like I'm on my own.

Well, it was the truth.

Bitter widow, lost widow, good widow. The word 'widow' didn't fit. It was a technical term. There was the future to consider. 'Now you're talking,' she mimicked Richard aggressively. 'Forwards. No slipping. Light a candle if you must.'

She would never again think of herself as a widow. What she was, was alone.

Was she looking after herself, Barrett wanted to know when she eventually followed him into the study. His question didn't come out right. Did he think she wasn't eating, that she wasn't washing herself? She was standing in the shower in the middle of the day until the water ran cold. She was eating ripe fruit from the large blue bowl on the living-room table, eating tinned fish over the sink, having biscuits and wine at her end of the couch. She didn't tell him any of this. It was none of his business.

'Yes.' She was looking after herself.

'They're good to you at work, are they? They're giving you the time?'

'Yes.' They were.

He flicked his head in a manner that suggested he was glad about this, but would not expect to fare well himself were he to suffer any class of trauma. 'Good. Good. You want to stay out of that place a while yet.'

She told him she intended to return to work on Monday week. He gave another twitch of the head. 'See how you go,' he advised. His words sounded weak to his own ears, but he persisted. 'Take all the time on offer, I'd say.'

Detective Barrett stood a long time in Richard Meadows' study staring one way, then another. He didn't seem to mind Gloria watching him. She sat on the edge of the old chaise longue with her fingers laced. What was he thinking, she wondered. Evidently, he was waiting for something significant to jump up and bite him.

Eventually, he spoke. 'Yours?' he said, indicating the laptop on the desk.

'No,' she replied. 'That's mine there.' She pointed to a second laptop, stored on a low shelf.

'You share this space?'

'Yes. But, as you can see, it's mostly Richard's domain. He was working from home in recent times.'

'Do you mind?' he asked, sitting carefully in the swivel chair and turning in to face the desk. 'You switched on his computer?'

'No. He left it on standby. It's always on standby.'

Barrett lifted the lid and the screen illuminated. Richard's files presented against a backdrop of the Brooklyn Bridge. 'No password required?'

'Coming out of sleep mode, no, but to start up, a password is required.'

'You have that?'

'No.' She might never turn it off, she told him. She didn't know.

'Do you mind?' he asked again. Now his fingertips were resting on the keyboard.

'Go ahead.' What did he think he might find? She told him she had looked at all the files, had opened all recent e-mails, so that she was familiar with his current, unfinished business. Barrett pretended he didn't hear. He made himself comfortable adjusting the flattened cushion under his backside.

'I'll just go ahead here,' he said belatedly. For over an hour he trawled through Richard's files,

PHILIP DAVISON

saying nothing. Sunlight tracked across the desk, showing up the particles of dust that had accumulated on the piles of paper and folders. Gloria lay back on the chaise and listened to Delius on headphones. Not once did Barrett look to his reclining host. Instead, he wrung little creaks out of the ageing swivel chair as an aid to concentration.

When, eventually, he was finished, he got up and made for the door as though leaving the room of a sleeping child. He offered the slightest of farewell gestures, which Gloria found unacceptable. She pulled off the headphones and sprang to her feet.

'I'm going,' he declared, freezing in his tracks.

'Well? Was that helpful?' she demanded.

'Yes. Thank you.'

'How was it helpful?' She didn't mean to sound inquisitorial, but, as court stenographer, she was used to the reticence of policemen, and she wanted more. She wanted a clear answer.

'There's nothing out of the ordinary, so far as I can tell – not that we expected . . . .'

There it was: that awful vagueness. 'All right, then.'

'I have a better picture now.'

'Of what?'

'His work. He was working steadily and consistently to the end.'

'You think?'

He put on his creased jacket. As he did so, he managed to turn the putting of one arm through the sleeve into a pointing gesture. 'That needs water,' he said, indicating the unwieldy weeping fig in the large pot in the corner of the study.

'You like plants?'

'I do, but I don't keep any. It's just that I noticed' – he threw a finger again in the direction of the parcels of yellowing leaves – 'and you don't want to see them suffer.'

'Of course not.' *This one is a misfit*, Gloria thought.

'I really should leave you now.'

'Of course you should,' she said distractedly, and showed him to the door. 'I didn't offer you anything. You could have tea, if you want.'

'No tea, thanks.'

She saw him all the way to the lift. Stood staring at the metal doors for some time after they had closed and the lift had descended.

16

Barrett didn't want her coming to the station if he could help it. With Mrs Meadows, a house-call was best. He would continue to conduct his interview in short sessions. He sensed that she liked him calling. She had not many people around her, he gathered. He presented himself at the Meadows' apartment again the following day and made his sheepish entrance.

'Mrs Meadows, would you be willing to view some CCTV images of your late husband,' he asked formally and politely. 'It might help with our investigation.'

'Yes, of course. What images are they?'

The detective had a small portable machine on which to play the recorded footage from one of the security cameras mounted in the underground car park of the apartment building. It showed Richard

Meadows entering the concrete refuse room with her chair, heaving it into one of the dumpsters, jumping in after it and, eventually, climbing out. It showed him ballooning left and right, looking about intensely and rubbing his injured shoulder before exiting. At first, Gloria was speechless. Without comment, the detective quietly played the piece again. This time, he froze the picture on Richard rubbing his shoulder.

'That must have been painful, all right,' he said – which wasn't helpful.

'Yes. It must.'

'What do you make of it, Mrs Meadows?'

'I don't know what to say.'

'I don't think he was – '

'Drunk. No.'

'A spontaneous event?'

'Yes. It appears to be . . . .'

'A sudden show of zeal. What about the chair?'

'I can't think what he was doing.'

The chair, Barrett was sure, was linked to their row. In uniform he had seen all sorts of wild behaviour when it came to domestic arguments. Possessions destroyed, clothes shredded or burnt, property thrown in the bin. He had become inured to it. He didn't know the chair had been returned and was in the bedroom, and Gloria didn't see the significance. So far as she was concerned, her late husband had done a rash and stupid thing, had quickly regretted it, and had retrieved her chair. There was no CCTV of Richard returning. Theirs was an old apartment block. The residents committee had paid for the installation of security cameras in the car park, in the utility rooms and at the rear fence. The heavy double doors at the main entrance were secure, and the intercom gave clean, crisp images. No additional camera had been installed here – the door through which Richard had returned with the chair.

'He doesn't look happy, mind,' said Barrett.

'No.'

'Frustration, do you think? I'm sorry to ask.'

'Yes. Maybe frustration.'

He unfroze the image. Let it play until Richard exited the refuse room. Froze it again on the frame that best favoured Richard's face. 'A man under some pressure, would you say?'

'It's the pain in his shoulder.'

'Impressive jump. Richard kept himself fit?'

'Well, yes. But he didn't go to any gym.'

'Concerned about his condition, no doubt . . . .'

'What are you saying?'

'Some with his condition are very cautious, but evidently your husband was not one of those. He was an active man.'

'Well . . . .'

'Out on sites with his job. Active in the physical world.'

'When he had work.'

'He was out of work in recent times?'

'He was doing some consultancy work.'

'Yes. I saw from his files.'

'He was applying for a post.'

'A man of his skill is always in demand, I'm sure. He wasn't . . . anxious, you tell me?'

'Depressed, you mean?'

The detective offered only the slightest inclination of the head.

'Down, maybe,' Gloria admitted.

'I don't wish to pry, but you know that I must have a clear sense of Richard's state of mind at the time of his disappearance.' It was his third visit, but

Detective Barrett had made scant acknowledgement of Gloria's job as a stenographer, someone well used to ribbons of intimate detail provided by strangers.

'I know what it is you're doing,' she said plainly.

'I'm sorry for this.'

'Don't be.' Her voice sounded bitter. That hadn't been her intention.

The detective inclined his head in the opposite direction. 'In time I hope to be able to answer all your questions.'

'Are you going to play those pictures again?' Gloria asked.

'No.'

'Can you leave the disc with me?'

'I'll keep it safely, Mrs Meadows. Can we talk again, soon?'

Gloria nodded tearfully. She could scarcely rise to her feet to see Barrett to the door, such was her response to the CCTV images of Richard. After he had left she found that her muscles were tense from rehearsing Richard's leap into the dumpster. She couldn't so much as shake her head. She just stood in the quiet, eyes tightly shut, teeth clenched, until her muscles began to ache and she felt their strength leaving her.

Action.

She could have a clear-out. That would be good. She could act on that. Offer his clothes to friends. No. His clothes to Oxfam. Make his workroom her workroom, where she might sit and read and roll out her yoga mat: better to have the wooden floor than bedroom carpet underneath.

She had thought that if the dead were to make contact across the divide, they might soften the shock by making the first pass via the telephone. Richard would approve of her deleting his number from her mobile phone. She could do that.

In the end, she vacuumed the place from top to bottom, not forgetting the Persian prayer-rug outside the hall door. She cleaned out the fridge, gathered up his medicines and his shaving gear: all that would be going in the dumpster after Richard. Before the sky fell down she opened a pricy bottle of Bordeaux and drank it all, then went to bed without immediate regret.

17

'All right,' Gloria said aloud, 'let's see you do something really brave.' Step into the lift, take that journey down to the bin-room to show that you care.

So, she did it. She left the door to the apartment unlocked and made her descent. She moved slowly past their parking space, looked hard into the emptiness, but there was nothing she could learn from it. There was no meaningful trace that she could discover. The car was burnt and gone. So, too, was Richard.

Gloria tried to remember what it was like to sit in the car, to drive it, to be driven in it. What came to mind was the sound of the windscreen wipers in the wet. They needed to be replaced.

She had put the car out of her mind; consigned its burnt husk to Detective Garda Barrett's care. He was preoccupied with it. He had spent a long time just staring at her set of car keys; staring as if they might speak. He was thinking about this and other acts of destruction, she supposed, while he brushed his teeth or lay in his bed at night.

The insurance payout on the car made her fret. She wasn't ready to drive again, despite encouragement from friends. What would she do with that sum of money if she didn't put it towards buying another car? Go on an extended holiday by herself? Take a friend, any friend who would go; take her mother? She didn't want that.

You're on your own, girl. A Marks & Spencer basket on a Friday night. Investigate any new lines on the shelves. Slippers at nine o'clock.

Gloria entered the bin-room half expecting to find her husband there, dead and alive. She stood in the concrete room with large bins on three sides of her. Stood where he had stood before launching himself.

Hello Richard. Me.

Nothing came back. She studied the junk in one corner that didn't get put in the bins: the glass top of a coffee table, an ironing board, an office printer, a box television set. There were places to dump such things.

She listened to water travelling in pipes above her head. She heard the distant whirr from the lift-shaft. She hoped it wasn't her friend, Fidelma, because she wasn't ready to talk today. She glanced over her shoulder. It was old Billy going out for one of his runs. She heard the creak of the electric gate to the car park opening at what always seemed to be half-speed. Even old Billy had to temper his running so as not to have to stop on his exit. When she turned her attention back to the bin-room, she stepped towards Richard's chosen dumpster. The smell wasn't too bad. He mightn't have smelt bad getting out.

She looked into the bin and, with a little bow of her head, made an altar of it.

'I'm sorry,' she said, then turned to leave. She noted the CCTV camera that was mounted on a cement girder beyond the open door. It was one of the new models, a dark little thing with a ring of ultra-red pin lights. She hadn't noticed it there before being introduced to its work. It was right that the detective had taken away his player and disc, Gloria decided.

'Sorry,' she whispered again as she passed under the eye. Though she was not feeling at all brave, it was the first of a number of walks she would take in Richard's name.

18

Gloria found a boarding pass for a London–Dublin flight folded in a shirt pocket. She was putting the shirt to her face when she felt the card in the breast pocket.

She studied it, but could give no detail to the basic scenarios she imagined. Richard had gone to London to . . . visit a friend. Who? He liked London. It was a place to go in a crisis. A place to get lost. To start something. Start what?

Maybe he had gone to see his Trinity College friend, Sam? She had a number for Sam. Poor old Sam had given it to her after the funeral. But wait: Sam had left London for a post in the U.S. That one they used to hang out with – Nicola – she went to London with Sam, but Sam went to New York by himself. Broke up with Nicola, according to

Richard. She might still be in London. Had he gone to her? Richard never thought much of her.

They had liked going to London together, she and Richard. Some piece of human scaffolding collapsed inside her. She couldn't put flesh on any speculative proposition.

She didn't do it immediately, but later that day she rang her detective.

'Mrs Meadows. What can I do for you?'

'It's probably not important, but I found a British Airways boarding pass in my husband's pocket. A flight from London to Dublin. For the time we're looking into.'

'Let's not talk on the phone.' It wasn't convenient for Barrett, but he offered to call to her apartment immediately.

'If you think it might shed some light.'

'We'll see.' Detective Garda Jarleth Barrett liked Gloria Meadows, liked her melancholy eyes, her slim shoulders, her tangled hair, her delicate complexion. He wanted to acknowledge her sadness and the sudden incompleteness of her life, but he didn't dare. He was surprised at the effect she had on him, but he couldn't let that show.

Did she want him calling? She wasn't sure. 'Perhaps you can find out more. I don't want to waste anybody's time.'

Gloria agreed to a prompt interview. She looked around and saw the mess that she had created, with piles of displaced clothes and personal effects. When Barrett buzzed from the lobby she came down and took him and the British Airways boarding pass to the café across the street, where they sat in a window seat.

'As I said, I don't want to waste your time.' In truth, Gloria was glad to speak again to somebody official.

'That's clear to me.'

She slid the flimsy card over the table-top. Barrett studied the boarding pass.

'Something unexpected?' he asked.

'Yes.'

'Never mentioned?'

'No. Never.'

'But he goes to London regularly, for his work?'

'Occasionally. I'd always know when he was going.'

Barrett nodded gravely. 'Just the one, you found?' he mumbled. 'You found no other?'

'No.'

'There was no ticket?'

'Not that I could find. I did look.'

'You told me before, when he left the apartment – after you had words – he didn't take a bag . . . .'

'No. He didn't.'

'Didn't come back to fill a bag?'

'I've checked.'

'You've checked.'

'I've looked. All our luggage bags are where they should be.'

'A light canvas bag, or the like . . . ?'

'I have checked.'

'What do you make of it yourself, Mrs Meadows – his trip to London?'

'It doesn't really have anything to do with him being knocked down, does it?'

'What I mean is, what do you make of his going to London?'

'He ran away.'

'Without a word.'

'Yes.'

'He doesn't want to come home. Not yet. He decides to make a visit.' Barrett gave a leading shrug.

'I can't think who he was visiting, if that's what you're asking. 'We have friends there, but there's no one I can think he'd visit without my knowing.'

'In that emotional state . . . .' He seemed to be indicating the basement car park of the apartment building where the bins were kept. He shrugged again. Gloria didn't like the shrugging.

'Look, we had a row – hardly a row. Call it a temporary falling-out. I imagine Richard was upset when he left the apartment . . . .'

'But you left before him,' he confirmed.

'Yes. We were both upset. I'm sorry. I *am* wasting your time here.' She looked at his brimming cup in a way that indicated it was time to drink coffee. She took a sip from hers; he was compelled to take several gulps in succession, though he broke to say: 'You've done exactly the right thing.' When he had finished scalding his mouth, Barrett briefed Gloria on the investigation to date – which was little more than informing her of procedural matters. Nothing new; nothing that she didn't already know. She listened dutifully, but his words soon fell away. She took in his face. A boy easily led, she thought, who had grown into an inhibited teenager, who had grown into a not easily fooled man.

'Didn't bring a bag, I expect, because he didn't know he was going, given the state of his mind.'

'Something like that.'

'He did what he did in the basement . . . .'

'He jumped in the dumpster.' Now *she* was extending *his* words. It made her uncomfortable.

Barrett nodded and squirmed a little in his chair. 'Then . . . took off. That would make sense. He flew to London – and who knows what . . . ?'

Here was that studied vagueness cops used as a method of winkling out further information. Gloria had nothing to add.

'We've seen the CCTV footage,' he continued. 'We know from his behaviour . . . .'

He changed gear, but preserved the musing tone. 'For what it's worth, Mrs Meadows, in my experience odd behaviour usually isn't quite so odd once we know what has caused it.'

Now she saw it: his lack of experience, his covering with received wisdom.

'Once we have the context,' she added darkly.

'Exactly,' he replied.

She had seen policemen in court perform like this. Usually they turned out to be extremely cunning. This one, however, had something in the eyes that let her warm to him, despite the shrugging, and his eagerness to finish her sentences. Perhaps he, too, had suffered a great and untimely loss.

He broke her introspection by pointing out the window. 'There's somebody waving at you,' he said.

'Where?'

Fidelma was giving a tight little wave of solidarity from the opposite pavement. Gloria readily returned the gesture. 'My neighbour.'

Detective Garda Barrett gave a polite wave, too – which was unnecessary and somewhat awkward.

'Her name is Fidelma,' Gloria said, to save the detective from himself. 'She's a friend.'

He let a flash smile fall quickly from his face. He struggled to regain his concentration. 'Could I ask you to think about why he might have travelled to London? It may, of course, have nothing to do with your husband's . . . accident.'

The conversation had gone full circle. Gloria's eyes grew more distant. Neither of them was going to drink any more coffee. 'You want to catch up with your friend,' Barrett said, extending a hand.

'Yes,' she replied. That wasn't true, but she rose to her feet.

'I'll be in touch soon,' he assured her.

'I'll think about London.' Gloria was already sliding away from the table, leaving the policeman to pay.

19

A review of Richard Meadows' credit-card transactions showed the purchase of the one-way air ticket from London Heathrow to Dublin. The record also showed the purchase of a sea-ferry ticket, Dun Laoghaire to Holyhead, two days earlier. Barrett checked ticket purchases on either side of the Meadows' transactions from the same credit-card machine for the London flight, to see if any connection might be made. Nothing significant presented itself. A family of four on the previous transaction; a businessman taking a connecting flight on the following transaction.

On the ferry ticket, Meadows had paid for two fares and a car. Not his car. Barrett found that the car was registered to one Virginia Coates. Drinks purchased on board with Virginia Coates' credit card. With her credit-card information, he was able to get her telephone number. This number cross-checked with Meadows' call log.

Detective Garda Barrett rang Virginia Coates, introduced himself, gave her the sad news of Richard Meadows' demise. She was shocked. He didn't tell her of his suspicions, just that Mr Meadows had been found on the roadside. it wasn't a full interview. That would follow later. He listened carefully.

'But what happened?' Virginia Coates asked. She seemed to have little or no air in her lungs.

'We don't know.' Barrett weighed heavily on the full stop. 'You knew Mr Meadows well?' he asked presently.

She knew what he was asking. Yes, she admitted, she knew him well.

'He went with you to London?'

'Yes.'

'For a short break?'

'Well, actually, I'm working here. I'm based here now.'

That wasn't the answer in code. It was a deflection of sorts. That was to be expected. As little more detail was forthcoming, Barrett changed gear: 'You had an ongoing relationship with Richard?'

'Yes,' she answered, without hesitation. There was a brief silence, followed by a suppressed sob.

'I see.' Barrett's voice was flat, non-judgmental.

'An accident, you're saying? Not his heart?'

Not a heart attack, Barrett told her. He give a timeline and location report. 'I'm sorry,' he concluded simply. She was grateful for this small acknowledgement. 'How long had you known him?'

She told him that she had known Richard as a boy, that they had met again recently. Barrett sensed that she was about to launch into biographical detail. He didn't want that now. He preferred to let the news sit. Let her think about his investigation, see if it alarmed her. See if, when he called again, she mounted a vigorous tactical defence, or remained upended. 'I would like to talk again.'

'Yes. I understand. How is his wife?'

'You know Mrs Meadows, perhaps?'

'I haven't met her.'

'You and I will talk in confidence.'

'In confidence. Yes.'

He'd be ringing again soon to arrange a face-to-face interview, he told her.

★

The insurance people had been on to Gloria. The mortgage would be paid off. The life-cover policy would provide a lump sum. It was thanks to her that the policy would pay out well. Had it been left to Richard, it would have been an altogether more frugal arrangement. Richard, now you see.

It felt vaguely fraudulent, but Gloria meticulously studied the terms, conditions and listed benefits accrued to the surviving spouse. She wasn't afraid of a little velvet, as her mother would put it: a little prosperity. She knew how she might invest and spend the money, but that didn't track how she might spend the rest of her life without her Richard.

She put on the white hard-hat Richard wore to building sites to study the insurance documents. Reading the policy made her want to get drunk. Instead, she fall into a deep sleep on the couch. She didn't hear Fidelma knocking on her door.

At home that same evening, after a tiresome telephone conversation with his brother, Barrett put on

Sibelius – something the widow Gloria might like. He went to bed early, allowed himself half an hour to think about the Meadows case.

The location chosen for dumping Richard Meadows didn't show much planning, expertise or dark wisdom. Barrett was moving in the direction of manslaughter, a malicious, but unintended, killing, and a panicked disposal of the body, the remains being ferried in Meadows' own car and dumped before the car was taken to the other site and burnt. The torching of the car was, he was sure, improvised at short notice.

He had already made enquiries among Meadows' friends, former employers and colleagues for any indication of grudges, personal disputes – anything that might be the basis for blackmail. Purposefully vague, even clumsy, enquiries, where he thought it prudent.

Nothing significant presented. He knew that sometimes, there was a delay. Somebody needed to be spooked.

20

Gloria wasn't sure what the phone call was about, not even when he said: 'By the way, does the name "Virginia Coates" mean anything to you, Mrs Meadows?'

'No. Why? Who is she?'

'Somebody who enquired about your loss. A friend from your husband's childhood.'

'I don't know her. Should I speak to her?'

'No need. You leave that to me. We're just being thorough.' Barrett had decided he would say nothing more to Gloria on the matter for now. There was digging he could do before upsetting her further. He would tell her about her husband's affair at a later date. He would tell her and linger a while to reassure her. He could bear witness, albeit in a modest way. She understood the value of bearing witness. If she let him stay, they might talk a while about her music.

★

The two-sided conversations about priorities, compromises and naked desire Gloria used to have with herself in the bathroom, she could now have anywhere in the apartment, but the bathroom had, if anything, become the essential transponder box.

Calls from friends and colleagues had subsided. It was understood that she didn't want to be shadowed. Later, there would be trips to the theatre, and dinner parties. She might join a book club, return to yoga classes, become a Friend of the National Gallery, but for now, she wanted time to herself. Today, she felt she was hiding away, holding her breath so that she could knit her insides back together. She couldn't have that. *Time to get out*, she thought, sitting on the toilet lid and staring into the shower pan. *Time to get on your feet*.

She rose very early in the morning, dressed for the outdoors, and began a long walk from her apartment to the South Bull Wall, a journey that would take her out into the middle of the bay. The tramp to the coast was as she imagined it would be, but took more time than she had anticipated. No matter. At Irishtown she rested a while and watched taxis and heavy-goods vehicles charging to the port tunnel. Pressing on, she crossed back and forth on the industrial neck of service land that led to the wall. This, too, took very much longer than she had expected, having visited here only in the car; it made her anxious. She was afraid that a prowling van or lorry would pull up beside her. She had her phone with her, but who would she call?

She alerted Jesus.

South Bank Road, White Bank, Pigeon House and on through the bends: south, east, north, east, north, and finally east again and on to the wall. Nothing bad happened. She was surprised at the calmness in this exposed place. Stumbling on the uneven surface that the old granite blocks presented was oddly reassuring. The Liffey flowed out on one side; the tide came in on the other. There was no glugging or lapping that she could hear. Even the gulls were, for now, mute. It was a flat, grey morning. The air was cool and salty. A rusty blue and white cargo ship passed her with a thudding engine noise and slid out to sea.

She nodded to two old men, pink and blubbery against the white wash of the Half Moon Swimming Club, but she talked to no one. She had no cogent flights of thought. She removed her woollen hat, unbuttoned her coat, let her pockets take the weight of her hands. *Don't walk on broken ground with your hands in your pockets*, she heard Richard chant. *Fuck off*, she replied with an easy softness.

Her fear of being attacked had passed. This wasn't tough, she reminded herself. Going down to the bin-room was tough. When she arrived safely at her destination, she pressed both palms firmly against the sloping red walls of the Poolbeg lighthouse. She had managed to reduce the gap between her physical tiredness and her emotional exhaustion.

Already, the wind was picking up. There were others now on the Bull Wall, coming in her direction. Two Chinese fishermen, who had bounced on their bicycles all the way to the lighthouse, dismounted and began assembling their long rods. They gave Gloria the slightest of nods, which she matched. Then, belatedly, she broke her silence with a booming 'Morning.' Both men nodded again, this time more emphatically.

'Morning,' one mumbled into a small lunchbox that was filled with bait.

And what was that? It was the kick that came with beginning something late. Gloria hadn't thought about the walk home. She took off for home with a start, determined to wear herself out.

On the tramp back along the wall, she was assailed by thoughts of Richard and his wandering, his ranging into such unfamiliar terrain, which Gloria took to be a measure of his upset – what she had come to recognise as disaffection. She could not let that be the end of it. She had been keeping at bay her need to know exactly what had happened, leaving it to the police to report to her, but now it was overwhelming. Might she have kept him safe by having not left the apartment that evening? By answering calls. She thought about a driver seeing a man in the roadway, about not being able to stop in time, then driving on. She could imagine it clearly. It was as vivid and egregious as the CCTV images of

Richard in the bin-room. She saw her poor stricken husband through the stranger's windscreen squint into the headlights the instant before impact. 'Stop.' But there was no stopping.

Her sense of purpose quickly drained, and suddenly she felt tired and hungry. On Bath Street she got in a taxi, but the thought of going home directly gave her a cramp. She wanted distraction. She had the driver take her through Ringsend and on to the city centre. She needed to buy food.

Gloria had taken to shopping in a Chinese supermarket. It was at Fidelma's suggestion. Though she didn't say it, she knew Fidelma went there to meet men of a certain age. Men who cooked for themselves and took a bit of trouble. She liked cooking Chinese and Indian food for herself. She could strike up a casual conversation and not feel exposed. She wasn't suggesting this for Gloria, of course, but now that Gloria was on her own she could explore as she explored. She liked the jars with a photograph of the chef or the company head on the label. *Smart move*, Fidelma thought. There wasn't such emphasis on sell-by or best-before dates. That was good for a person living on her own. Fidelma had not actually brought home any man from any supermarket as yet, though she had had a number of encounters. She didn't feel under pressure. She was exercising patience and was quietly optimistic.

None of this meant much to Gloria, but she went there now. It was inappropriate, she thought. That was a help.

She wandered up and down the aisles reviewing her life with Richard until a handsome young man spoke to her – something about yams. She found herself behaving more like Fidelma than Fidelma, just for the hell of it. There was a certain disconnected pleasure to it.

When she opened her cupboard now, she had successful Chinese entrepreneurs staring out at her, the men serious, the women serious and smiling. She had opened most of the jars and a few of the tins to use a little of their contents. They could be in her cupboard a very long time and still do their stuff, she supposed, but what to do with the yams and that polystyrene pallet of magnificent red chillies? She could pool with Fidelma, of course, but Fidelma was fully stocked.

21

Gloria dreamt that her fingers froze and meta-morphosed into claws, which she had to show the judge and excuse herself, first in English, then in Irish, French and Italian. The judge halted the murder case to let Gloria through to her private antechamber. She was savvy enough to see that Gloria couldn't turn the door handle by herself, and did it for her. 'Stay in here,' she ordered. 'I don't want anybody seeing the state of you.' The be-clawed Gloria glimpsed her mother taking her place in court in front of the judge. Her mother was all bangles and rings and smiling red lips when she presented her scrawny hands to the judge for inspection. Gloria woke before approval was given.

Her first day back in court was a Friday. For her it proved uneventful. Colleagues treated her kindly. The case in Courtroom 7 had no frenetic closed-captioning; no translation was required; there was no video depositions. However, Gloria was afraid she wouldn't be able to concentrate, that she would have to report herself to the court clerk and to the judge. In the event, she coped. In fact, the proceedings had the uncanny smoothness of a vivid narrative dream, which in itself was a signal of distress.

She had a bottle of water for her lunch. She took a short walk in the Phoenix Park, then hurried back to her post. When the 'all rise' command came, she faltered. The day was already too long. There had been too much deliberate talk. She yearned for the night, when she could get out again and walk and be guided by the incidental sounds of the city and the blessed quiet, when she could shake off the dream-state of her real-time reporting and be wholly alert.

She fell asleep on the couch; woke on the edge of her bed, one startled foot searching for a shoe. It was half past midnight when Gloria stepped out of the apartment building and stood on the pavement, looking up into the night sky. Why was the moon in black and white?

I think I feel the earth spinning, she told Richard. *What do you make of that?*

That can't be good, came the reply.

No, she confirmed.

Does it make you dizzy?

Not yet. But I'm nodding from the ankles.

Emotional gyroscopics. That's what you're experiencing. I'm watching you now. I don't see physical movement.

I'm telling you what I feel.

Clock or anti-clock?

Clock.

You feel the earth spinning and *you're rotating from the ankles?*

Yes.

Can't do anything for that. I'll keep watch.

'You're useless to me,' she shouted into the night, more loudly than she had intended. Somebody came to a window two floors above the café. That brought Gloria's eyes down to street level, looking left and right for any sign of comfort. The lights in the café were burning, but the shutter was down. They were cleaning up.

She told Jesus she was out again and set to walking. Gloria hadn't taken up the offer of counselling, because Jesus was her counsellor. She spoke; he listened. For the record, she wanted to make several declarations. First, there would be no hoarding of grief.

She would not hoard her grief. What else?

She would grieve, yes. She was grieving now, but . . .

Go on, Gloria, what else?

She would waste no time with regrets.

What regrets were these?

Her marrying Richard. There, she had said it. Having no children because of his negligible sperm-count. Letting him slacken on their plan to adopt until it was too late. Sacrificing, and for what? This crock who grew more distant and vague, this fool who had got lost and had died on her in a place he should never have been. What she had given up for Richard Meadows.

She paused to admit that there was a time each had sought to embrace the doubts and desires of the other. A time when they were drawn towards each other, the one thinking the other was standing in the heat and the light. There was a point where they had drawn level and were perfectly poised. That was when she had a family: her and Richard. When Jesus could see they were on their way together, and in the here and now.

When she crossed the river northwards on Beckett Bridge, she was thinking of the fractured plumbing throughout the city: all the leaks, big and small, the water sinking deep into the earth, the plumbers turning up late, not shaking their heads. The system would never be patched up, could never be fully patched here or in any other city, Richard had told her. It was part of the planet's finite and constant body of water, however we exploited it. We could only ask where the water was located at any given time.

The wind was playing on the surface of the Liffey and in the suspension wires of the bridge. It was lulling drunk sailors sleeping below the waterline, she imagined. Calling in the foxes. It had taken her some three hours to get here because she had, without temporal reason, walked, unchallenged and unmolested, the four sides of St Stephen's Green, Fitzwilliam Square and Merrion Square before going to the river.

She was now on the redeveloped North Wall, the financial district. Montreal, she thought – though she had never been to Montreal. Clean, nicely squared off, scrubbed quays with placid water, model trees, a tram, smartly dressed pedestrians with take-away coffees - a take-away coffee in the neighbourhood where she worked carried differently. There was a better class of seagull at this end. She could move down here. Be a stranger. From this place a person might go anywhere.

She walked in blocks again, alert and dumb – which was why, perhaps, she got a chill when she caught sight of herself in a plate-glass window. It wasn't her clothes or her demeanour that irked, but an unfamiliar expression. She was prompted to move on when another solitary figure on the far pavement appeared and slowed, to observe her.

She turned west and made her way along by the river, past the Customs House, to the desert that is O'Connell Street. As she turned the corner she glanced behind and caught sight of the man she had seen reflected in the plate-glass window. Not a youth, not an old man; not somebody shambling along, but walking with purpose. A fit, middle-aged man with floppy blond hair. He was dressed in a short coat, flannel trousers and trainers. He was keeping pace.

There were a few rowdy shouters stumbling her way. That didn't bother Gloria. It was part of what she was seeking out. She didn't avoid them. Didn't give them a wide berth, but pushed on through, inviting their slack-mouthed leers and soaring catcalls. She could brush with toppling drunks, even shake hands with huddled figures in doorways, and be on her way. She could have an affair behind Richard's back, Jesus told her. She could do that now and still be on her way.

It was the trainers that set her off. Could he really be following her?

She turned again, this time heading for the district where she worked. Between her place of work and her present position was the fruit-and-vegetable market. She could take refuge in the halls if she needed to, among familiar faces. She'd be safe there.

But she was still too early for the market men and women. It would be another half an hour before the halls were open. On a stretch of Mary's Abbey she paused for a moment, turned quickly, saw no one, found herself clutching her thumping heart.

God tempers the wind, said Maria, to the shorn lamb. Who said that? It wasn't from the Bible. Who was Maria? It was her own voice that spoke these words in her head. Where did she get them? This was something to fix on, instead of the business of putting herself in danger.

At the grand corner gate to the market halls she dodged to the right, slowed her pace, filled her lungs with the faint tang of over-ripe fruit. She determined she would make a square of it, then strike back across the river and head for home. If her legs gave out, she would hail a taxi. Left, left again on the redbrick corners. Somewhere in the jumble of adjacent lock-ups and warehouses she heard the rattle of a heavy shutter winding up on its roller. As she broke from the cover of the fourth corner she saw him again, advancing towards her, making no sound on his feet. His timing was unnatural. He was just yards away when he spoke.

'Are you all right?' he said in a soft voice. These few words struck physical dread in Gloria. She ran for all she was worth, until she thought she tasted blood and her legs had turned to jelly. She collapsed in a heap against the river wall. *Was she all right?* What could he see, that creepy blond-haired stranger in his coat and trainers? The encounter had sent her reeling, made her dizzy, made her feel sick in her soul. God damn Richard Meadows.

It was a bright, blowy morning. Nearly 7 AM. Cars flew by, their glass flashing the yellow morning light. She did something she had never done before: she went to an early house. She'd seen the painted notice on the parapet of a corner pub advertising a '7 AM opening', seen it as she passed on the elevated railway. She went there.

She needed a stiff drink. There were two solitary figures at the bar. Men who gave the impression they wouldn't be staying long, but would not be hurried.

'Morning,' the bartender said powerfully. 'What can I get you?'

Gloria searched for any sign of pity in his face. There was none. She ordered at the counter, then slid onto a bench seat. The one drink knocked her sideways, and she was grateful for that. She closed her eyes to let the light on her cheeks be her balm. Nobody would mind, she was sure, if she opened them again soon.

An hour later she took one step out of the doorway onto the pavement. She felt so weak she was afraid she might fall down in the road between cars and go under the wheels before she got to lie in her sorry bed. She waited to hail a taxi from where she stood.

22

'Look, it's time I came to see you.'

The phrasing and the intonation suggested that he had been torturing himself with the decision, but was finally taking action.

'Yes, Tom,' Gloria said, as though he had caught her naked on the stairs. 'Of course. I'd like that. It's long overdue.' *Long overdue*: what the hell was she saying? What kind of signal was she sending?

Tom was in her thoughts lately, it was true. Richard liked Tom, and Tom had always liked Richard. Gloria was sorry for Tom, and knew that he now felt sorry for her. They both had to get away from feeling sorry.

'Any time that suits,' he said, already in retreat. 'We could meet for coffee, if you like. Any time at all.'

Gloria marched up and down at her window with the telephone pressed hard to her ear. She heard herself inviting him for a meal. 'It's Chinese night,' she told him.

'That's good. I like Chinese. Want me to collect it?' He did well to cover his excitement.

No-no, she explained, she was preparing the food at home. Actually, she was thinking that lunch would be better.

'Wonderful. I'll bring something special.'

Oh God. What was she doing really? Poor Tom. Poor Gloria. Where had all the sparrows gone?

'When you say Chinese night . . . . We're having lunch, right?'

'Yes. Chinese lunch. Two o'clock.'

'That's fine. I don't want to get the time wrong.'

Gloria lifted her eyes to the mirror. Only the eyes were hers, with their smudged black rings. The body belonged to her mother. A good-looking mother, she had to admit. A woman with bobbed grey hair turning white, who would still flirt with the likes of Tom.

Change the hair, she thought, prodding her fingers through the thick of it. Its thickness afforded some protection in court. It seemed to absorb some of the excess alpha-waves. Getting the right cut would be a challenge.

Widow. She spoke the word aloud. Bag-lady potential, she thought. Best go to London for that. She'd be a good bag lady – if there was such a thing as being good at it. She would persist, is what she meant. She still had stamina. She had never been less than tenacious. Pity, in a way.

The longer she stood in front of the mirror, the less like her mother she appeared. She studied her reflection for a long time. *Change the hair*, she confirmed. No bob.

She saw that she had arched her back and was pushing her breasts out. She did not judge herself harshly. She ran the fingertips of one hand lightly down her throat, where the skin had started to sag. She had things to say to Tom that would excite them both, as she and Richard had once been excited. This had not been lost. He would be making an effort, too, no doubt.

She would try that burgundy lipstick, and be free with her talk.

★

Tom was late. While she waited, she soaked the roots of the weeping fig in Richard's study, then, in an extension of her spontaneous action, pruned it to extinction.

She knew that Tom's business wasn't doing well. He might be sued. Perhaps she could help with getting him the best legal counsel. Richard would want her to help him.

She and Tom were made of resilient stuff, she thought. More elastic than Richard. Perhaps there wasn't much active consoling to do. The one cancelling the other, as it were. Just a deep blue embrace, a tear or two, then open his bottle of fine wine – which he was certain to bring. She was back at the living-room window, looking down anxiously into the street.

Start with a firm embrace and the evening would be a simple success, even if the food she made was a disaster. Latecomers weren't in a position to complain.

Serving something bland or mediocre would be worse. In any case, what she had cooked didn't go with red wine. She must remember to make a fuss of the wine he had under his oxter.

'Sorry I'm late, Gloria,' he panted. 'Sorry, sorry.'

'That's all right, Tom.' She gave him a firm embrace and kissed him on the cheek.

'Mmm, lovely smell.'

Did he mean her or the lunch? Gloria didn't ask.

'What's that?' he enquired, looking in through the open study door at the pile of branches from a weeping fig.

'A mistake,' she replied bluntly.

Did she mean that having the fig tree was a mistake, or chopping off the branches? He didn't ask. 'Never mind,' he said. He wanted to sound enthusiastic, but he was reeling from his latest fiasco. 'They want the house,' he declared, following Gloria through to the kitchen. 'That's what has delayed me.'

'Your *house*. You're having to sell up?'

'No. The bank. They're taking it.'

'Dear God. Can't you reschedule the mortgage? Pay interest only?'

'Done all that.' He had two bottles of wine, one for each oxter. He handed them over.

'Oh.'

'We'll want one of them open right way. Let it breathe.'

'Of course.'

'Open them both, maybe . . . .'

'Bastards. Sorry to hear about the situation. If they put you on the street, you can stay here.'

'Can I?'

'No.'

He laughed, and so did she. She was surprised by her own offer. With both arms free now, he embraced her. Actually, it was more of a bear-hug. 'Gloria . . . Gloria . . . .' He sprang her free.

'What will you do?'

'I'll find a few quid, give them that, and renegotiate. That's what has me late. I was on the phone. Sorry.'

'You didn't buy this specially?' she asked, holding one bottle aloft.

'I have a few left. When that's gone, well . . . .'

He stepped in close again; this was more intimate than the bear-hug. 'How are you?' he asked, in something just above a whisper.

'I'm OK,' Gloria said, and blanched. They were both wildly self-conscious, but not feeling guilty, and that was thrilling. He nodded, broke into a broad smile and moved to take down two stem glasses from ranks on a nearby shelf. Gloria hesitated, seemed momentarily frozen.

'Show me what you have,' he said, pointing to the stove with a glass. 'You sit down and I'll serve.'

She did just that. 'I meant to say to you, Tom, that if you need legal advice I could recommend someone, I'm sure. I can ask.'

'Thank you so much,' he said, rooting for a corkscrew without asking. 'Have one.' He told her the name of his solicitor. 'She's not bad – so far. We'll see, won't we?'

Gloria tried to sound positive. She closed her eyes for the cork-pop. Opened them to watch her guest put the mouth of the bottle to his nose and inhale. 'I'm looking forward to this.'

There was a buzz from the intercom. Gloria lifted the receiver and saw on the small screen her mother lean into the camera lens mounted in the speaker-box. Gloria let out an impressive whinny.

'It's me, darling,' her mother announced militantly. 'Open the door.'

'Hell's bells.'

'Hell's bells,' Tom repeated. He hadn't heard that phrase in a long time.

'My mother.' For a moment it appeared that Gloria was stuck to the floor with daughterly exasperation.

The buzzer sounded again. 'I know you're there.'

'Aren't you going to let her in?'

'Of course I am.' She buzzed her mother into the building, went to the apartment door, swung it open and stood with one leg in the corridor to watch the entrance to the lift.

When the lift doors opened, her mother stepped out like a diva. She had this act she put on that suggested she wasn't sure which apartment her daughter and son-in-law occupied. She did her strange-place walk now, despite seeing Gloria positioned in her doorway.

'Hello, mother.'

'Hello, Gloria dear.' She had a Brown Thomas bag firmly crooked on one forearm, which temporarily masked the ancient crocodile handbag underneath. 'You're in,' she added pointedly.

'I'm in,' Gloria confirmed.

'Happy birthday, dear.' She held the bag out long before she reached the apartment door.

'Thank you, Iris.' She used her mother's given name in an attempt to even things up. It never worked. 'You really shouldn't have given it any thought.'

'Can't help it, can I? You're entertaining?' She gleaned this by the way her daughter was standing.

'As a matter of fact . . . .'

'I'm glad,' she said, abandoning her strange-place walk in favour of something more progressive. 'I won't be staying.'

Gloria took the Brown Thomas bag with a gracious smile and gave her mother a one-arm hug. 'Thank you,' she said again.

'How are you?' Iris asked. She wasn't about to settle for anything less than a heartfelt full embrace.

'I'm all right,' Gloria replied softly. She had told her as much on the phone the previous night. She knew that Iris was looking over her shoulder into the apartment to see who she had in there. Secretly, she had always thought that her mother was well set up for widowhood. Did her mother now think the same of her? 'Come in.'

'Are you sleeping?' her mother asked, moving ahead without hesitation.

Gloria's sleep was erratic. It didn't matter which side of the bed she slept on. When she slept, she didn't remember much about the sleeping – except that it saved her life. 'Yes, I'm sleeping.'

'That's my girl.'

'Mother, this is Tom.'

'Tom,' she repeated, as if testing the weight of the name, and finding it wanting.

'Pleased to meet you.'

'Gloria,' she said, abruptly switching, 'aren't you going to open your present?'

'I am.' Gloria fumbled with the black bow tired across the mouth of the striped bag, the ribbon her mother had double-knotted.

'It's her birthday,' Iris said, switching back. 'She didn't tell you, did she?'

'No. She didn't.'

'Happy birthday, my darling.'

For an instant, it sounded to Tom's ears that he was required to repeat the sentiment by rote. 'Happy birthday,' he said, wisely dropping the 'my darling', but substituting it with an awkward peck on the cheek.

'I saw you at the funeral,' her mother continued, her tone now suggesting *interloper*. 'Are you moving in?'

'How lovely,' Gloria interjected loudly, as she pulled the finest of cashmere cardigans from the bag, sending a wad of tissue paper fluttering to the floor. 'Thank you, Iris.'

It was clear to Tom that Gloria's sprightly eighty-two-year-old mother liked to fire her big guns first to see what would fall over. He was on to her. In fact, the encounter steeled his resolve. 'You did see me at the funeral. And no, I'm not moving in.'

'You're a friend of my son-in-law?'

'Yes.'

'Gloria invites *you* on her birthday, not her dear old mum. You can see I'm not offended. It's as it should be. No friends for back-up. Fair enough, I say. Not even what's-her-name from upstairs.'

'Fidelma.'

'A nice woman, Fidelma.'

'Iris. Please . . . .'

'Won't you sit down?' Tom asked, pulling out a chair.

'Sit down,' Gloria ordered.

'You needn't worry,' Iris said, sitting down, 'I'll not be staying. What's that you're cooking?'

'Stay,' Gloria insisted lamely. 'Have something to eat with us.'

'You'll not make a gooseberry out of me.' This, to anyone who might recognise it, was tacit approval.

'We're starting with dumplings.'

'Dumplings?' Iris said with incredulity. She wasn't about to let up on the drama.

They were then going to have noodles with crispy black bean chilli sauce, and chicken in fresh ginger with bok choy, mangetout, shallots and cashew nuts.

'Good God.'

'I'm really looking forward to it,' Tom remarked comfortably.

'Poor Richard,' Gloria's mother said, and suddenly burst into tears. Tom moved out of the way to let Gloria give Iris's shoulders a firm hug – which saw her rally quickly. 'What do you think happened, Tom? We don't know. The Guards don't know. What was he doing wandering in the middle of nowhere, the bloody fool?'

Tom had no idea. 'We must be patient.'

'Huh.' Gloria gave her mother a glass of water. 'Something stronger, and I'll be on my way.' She poured her a gin and tonic. 'We might never know,' Iris continued, making fierce eye-contact with her daughter and squeezing her wrist. Gloria had to look away. For a while the three were joined in a deep silence. It was Gloria who looked searchingly to the others. Her love for Richard was not for sharing, they must know.

'I'm sorry,' said Iris. 'Happy birthday, Gloria. Happy birthday, love.' She rose to her feet, this strong-willed, agile and inquisitive old bird, and pointed with her glass. There was just the slightest weakness in the hips that made her roll a little when she walked. You could see it now as she left the kitchen and made for the open study door. 'What's that heap? What have you done, dear?'

'I'm pruning,' Gloria said.

'I can do that for you.' She was weeping again, and drinking from her glass as she circled the pile of fig branches on her way to visit the jagged thing that was left standing in the large ceramic pot.

Iris was so upset for Gloria and for herself, it wasn't difficult to get her to stay for lunch. Gloria had the extra place set at the dining table before her mother had agreed to it. Iris didn't want wine. She stuck with her gin and tonic. She didn't eat much, just picked at what was put on her plate. While the other two were still eating, she got up from the table, went to the piano and took a wad of sheet music from the piano stool. 'Still here,' she declared with a lamentable sigh.

These were scores from the Great American Songbook, she explained to Tom – songs her husband used to play at this very piano, songs he would sing to her.

'And to me,' Gloria added.

'We were happy together, weren't we?' It was as though she sought the confirmation from Tom, not her daughter.

'Yes,' Gloria answered gladly. 'You were.'

'That was before I put him in the home for the bewildered. I had to, you understand.'

Tom nodded. He understood.

'*I'll* not be going in,' she assured him. 'They won't have *me* reciting the alphabet every morning. I wouldn't go. Would I, Gloria?'

'No. You wouldn't.'

'The three of us here are happy together,' Iris declared, as though it were a revelation. She had consumed too much to drive. She was really quite drunk. Ready to start a sing-song. Gloria said she would call a taxi. 'I've told her to take my car, now that their one is gone,' Iris told Tom. 'I don't need it much. I've enough for taxis, haven't I, dear?'

'You do. If I need to borrow your car – '

Her mother jumped in: 'Take it,' she boomed.

'If I need it, I'll be on to you. Have you anything in your fridge?'

Gloria's concern was dismissed with a wave of the hand. 'Tom, dear, will you bag that mess in the study, and put it in the bin?'

'I will.' And he did. He and Gloria packed the fig branches into two large refuse sacks. He then slung them on his shoulders, and took them down in the lift to the bin-room, where he toppled them into an empty dumpster.

The white sap made his hands stick to the steering wheel for the journey home. He was a little drunk, too. Drunk and confused – though he didn't know about what. Not his money troubles. That was something separate. It had to do with the compassionate visit: that's what had him so charged.

As best he could, he kept a steady speed all the way back to the bank's house.

23

Several days of rain showers had made Gloria think that the plants on her winter garden balcony didn't need water. In fact, she hadn't watered them in two weeks or more. It was only now that she saw they were in a sorry state. But she could bring them back, she was sure.

Maybe she should just chuck them. Start with a new lot. Get a new weeping fig for the study, not let it grow from a plant into a tree.

She made a hell of a mess, but got the balcony plants into plastic sacks, got the sacks down to the bin-room, got them into a dumpster. She went back up to the apartment, had her wine and biscuits, then went to church. She hadn't been there since her husband's funeral. She went early, arriving just as the doors were unlocked. She knelt in a pew and prayed moderately for her own salvation in this life, and hard for Richard's spirit to go forwards and to settle. Could Richard Meadows, a Protestant atheist, please be shunted into the domain that lay beyond disbelief, as he was, no doubt, still in denial.

She left the church before the service began. She slipped out through one of the heavy swing doors with a nod to the smiling reverend, who seemed to be holding out his hand to her as he approached from the vestry.

The reverend didn't follow her into the open. She was glad to get the wet gravel under her feet again, to feel the mist on her face. The wine she had drunk on the couch made he want to pee. She peed in what she called the canon's bushes, then had to wait to let the first parishioners for the evening service pass. She had never done the like before. She didn't feel bad about it, though she supposed that she should.

She was now ready for a long walk through the cool, earthy evening. The praying for Richard wasn't enough. This would be her most ambitious night-walk yet. What had begun with a tentative journey to the bin-room would now end with a pilgrimage to the place where Richard's body had been found.

What precisely had happened, and where? She had faith that she would be told. Detective Barrett and his colleagues were doing what they could to establish just that. In time, they would give her the discoverable facts. Right now, she was compelled to walk to that place where his journey had ended.

She had got Barrett to show her the precise location on a large-scale map. She had had him describe the immediate geography – which he dutifully did, as he recognised her fierce desire to bear witness.

'Would you like me to take you there?' he asked eventually, but she declined.

'There's no need,' he assured her.

But here she was, and glad to be on her way, feeling only intermittent bouts of trepidation. She calculated that it would take her some three hours on foot if she didn't lose her way. She had been out in the streets in the night for as much, but that was wandering; this was different. It would be the same hike home, whenever the indeterminate time spent there had passed.

Setting off from the doors of the church was odd, but it added to her resolve – which had been building with all her hours of melancholic lingering in the apartment. That wine she had drunk on the couch was churchy, come to think of it.

Gloria told Jesus what she was doing. Her feet were ahead of her. They took her under drooping branches, past illuminated shops and pubs to the Grand Canal, where they struck west. Idle locks, bulrushes, swans, floating plastic sacks, a burst bag of chips, an angry man exercising his miserable dog – 'Evening' – gurriers out on the skite: they were all a spur.

Wet, but it was not raining. Rain that wasn't rain. Something soft and premature that made the air thin and cool. Clouds had come down to rub the earth and condense there. Gloria was in a cloud. The wetting was good, she imagined. It was something she could easily endure. A person could sing a song and their spirits would be lifted.

But Gloria did not sing. She could only think of hymns, and that would not be right on this march. Sinatra, then, or John Lennon. She couldn't line up the lyrics. Instead, she took in her environment: the structures and fixtures, the lie of the land, the relationship of things.

There was a car dealership, carpet and tile warehouses on the near side of a narrow rise over railway tracks and canal. Beyond, on the flat industrial parkland, there were many more nondescript warehouses with loading bays, and a few bungs of neglected countryside. This was the place. She was looking for a triangular tract of scrubland with pylon wires straddling a grass bank that fell away towards the canal. There were no footpaths here. The far-off footpaths she could see in the industrial park were entirely deserted.

It had taken much more time than she had anticipated to get to this location. Now that she had arrived, she was both glad and afraid. Her fear was not for her physical safety, but that she could not make this a pilgrimage. Afraid, too, for what was to follow. She was not prepared for a solitary life, and not equipped, she felt, to make it otherwise. She couldn't bear talking to herself for any length of time when Richard was alive, much less now that he was gone.

She would sit a while; talk, if it came to her. Under her waterproof, she was wearing a dress she knew Richard liked. She opened her coat, that it might be seen.

And where exactly would she sit? On that rise, between a pylon and the ditch. Richard's ditch. She found a spot to cross by a culvert. She sat on her chosen patch. From there she could see the route she had come. The long, low rectangle of the illuminated window of the car showrooms, the regular intervals of smudge-light from lamp-posts. She was not addled, nor was she disorientated. Quite the opposite, in fact. But this was a forlorn place, and she was sorry for that.

What now, with the sodden ground under her behind and her knees gathered under her chin? She had not come to speculate. She had come to honour her husband. She spoke his name into the mist. 'I'm here,' she said, and suddenly felt utterly exhausted.

She saw that the next pylon was also close to Richard's ditch, and now that she studied the terrain, she decided that she was in the wrong spot. That other pylon was the true marker. She would go and sit there a while. She wanted to shoo Richard on, then go home and sleep until it was time to work. She would go to that other pylon, announce herself again, sit a while, then go home to bed. It was what he would have done.

So, she got up and picked her way along the uneven ground. She didn't see that the ditch turned back on itself before crossing under that second pylon. The fall was not great, but her landing was hard. She was sure she had broken her wrist.

There wasn't much pain at first. It was more the shock. She was able to climb out of the ditch and get onto the road near the railway line. 'Sorry,' she mumbled to herself. 'Sorry,' she called out, and began to pound in the direction of the city.

The pain came soon enough. Translucent bubble-worms wriggled across her corneas. She sat on a grass verge for fear of fainting on the road. The driver of an AA van stopped when he saw the huddle in the grass.

'Did you have a breakdown?' he called through his open window.

Gloria shook her head. He put on his hazard-lights and got out.

'What happened?' he asked, as he helped her into the passenger seat.

'I've been walking,' she said in a light whisper.

'Walking?' he echoed darkly.

'I slipped. I'm so tired, you see.'

'You get in there now.'

'Do you mind if we don't speak?'

She seemed to be holding out her wrist for him. He looked at it. Didn't dare touch. 'You hold tight, love. I'll have you there in no time.' He didn't say where *there* might be. He was going to drive her to Accident and Emergency. She didn't mind him buckling her safety belt.

He radioed his dispatch and took off over the humpback bridge with a lurch and a bounce.

'Sorry,' she said, on the edge of consciousness.

'No bother,' he said. 'No bother,' he repeated.

The nearer they got to their destination, the faster he drove.

24

'You dozy mare,' Fidelma said. 'Don't you know I would have gone with you? Driven you there. Been with you.'

'Yes,' Gloria replied shakily. 'Thank you. It was important: I wanted to be in that place by myself.'

'I could have stayed in the car.' Both women had a grip on her, one at either elbow. Gloria's mother had no qualms about clutching the slung arm firmly.

'I did what I wanted to do,' Gloria replied. She was embarrassed, open now to a charge of dizziness, if not lunacy. That had to be dispelled.

Two intertwined peels of infectious laughter, one male, one female, echoed across the underground car park. 'There's a lot of happy couples in this building,' Gloria said. 'In this city,' she added. It was the painkillers talking.

'Not us, dear,' her mother pointed out. 'Not at the moment. We must make do.'

'We're a right pair, the three of us,' Gloria declared, as they entered the lift. It was their turn to laugh. They were silent for the ascent, and for the walk on the corridor to Fidelma's apartment. Gloria knew that her mother was in shock, and that this was delaying the extended rebuke that would surely come.

'You have it lovely,' Iris said, taking in her surroundings. It was smaller and more cluttered than the Meadows' flat, but immediately comfortable.

'Thank you. Now, sit down. I'll do the rest.'

'Here we are,' Gloria said, while Fidelma was in the kitchen getting the drinks and food. She thought she might draw her mother out, get the lecture over and done with.

'Here we are,' her mother repeated, putting the tone right.

'Safe and sound.'

'Yes, well, we'll see if you've stopped your foolishness. Have you heard more from the Guards?' Might her daughter be keeping something from her that would explain her taking off into the night?

'Nothing new.'

'I should talk to that so-called detective.'

'Mother, just let them do their job.'

'They won't get any discouragement from me.'

'Just leave them be. They've enough to deal with.'

'Huh.'

The three women gathered respectfully at a small coffee table with their food and drinks. They sat forwards, mother and daughter on a baggy floral couch, the host on a matching armchair.

Iris leaned slightly sideways. 'You were left there for an hour or more on the side of the road, suffering.'

'I wasn't.'

'No one would stop. There are no good Samaritans out that way. None anywhere these days.'

'I wasn't there long. A man in a van stopped. He was very kind. He took me all the way to St Vincent's.'

'You could have been raped. An ambulance should have been called.'

'Mother, please . . . .'

'You could be dying on a crowded street, and nobody would lift a finger.'

'It was my fault. I wasn't careful enough, and I fell.'

'For God's sake, what did you think you were doing out there in the cold and wet?'

Gloria didn't answer. Her lower lip began to tremble. Fidelma came in sweetly: 'She was paying her respects.'

This formal phrase halted Iris for a moment, who leaned across to clasp her daughter's free hand, but then sprang back in her chair and announced: 'I'm disappointed in my particular branch of humanity.' It was a crude attempt to make less of her gall, but Gloria was on to her.

'Which branch would that be?'

'This locale.'

'What, this city?'

'And environs. It's catching.'

'That's a bit previous, wouldn't you say, mother?'

'Nothing previous about it. I'm *very* – '

'Very disappointed. In the general population. You've told us.'

'You gave me a fright, Gloria. You want to do me out of existence?'

'I'm sorry.'

'She *is* sorry, Iris,' Fidelma put in.

'The things that happen . . . .'

'Stop your worrying,' Fidelma urged. 'Will you not have one of these?' she asked, offering a plate of sharp-cut triangle cheese-and-ham sandwiches.

Iris pursed her lips and shook her head. 'Gloria will have one,' she volunteered.

Gloria took a sandwich, and bit into it. 'Very nice, Fidelma,' she said sorrily.

Her mother hadn't finished with her caustic show of relief. 'They ate a lot,' she observed presently. Despite Gloria's mad hike, her broken arm, her hellish stint in A&E, they were all thinking about the killing of Richard.

'Who ate a lot?' Gloria wanted to know. She was in for some heavy criticism, she was sure. Something inappropriate. Something twisted.

'Your guests. At the afters.'

'I can't believe you'd say that, mother.'

'There was nothing left. I'm glad. It must be a good thing. You were there, Fidemla. You saw.'

'You did a splendid job looking after everybody, Iris.'

'At one point I thought I wouldn't have enough food for everyone.'

'Thank you again for your effort, Iris,' Gloria said tightly, 'but it wasn't about you, remember?'

'Funerals do that to some people,' Iris continued. 'I can never eat a thing. She pointed with a thumb. 'Her Tom couldn't put away enough. Sandwiches, sausage rolls, canapés. Especially the canapés.' She could see that her daughter was tearful – which was entirely fitting. 'I was glad to be busy,' she said to Fidelma, but really she was addressing Gloria. She would explore the subject of the Tom fellow another time. Fidelma would have his cards marked, she was sure. She'd talk to her.

But she couldn't leave it alone. After a brief lull, she said: 'You're quick off the mark, I must say.'

Gloria rapidly made herself available. 'What are you saying?'

'You're right, of course. I knew there was something going on when you wouldn't come over to me for your birthday dinner. She's a dark horse, this one,' Iris said, deferring to Fidelma. 'You'll know that. She has her friend over on her birthday. You weren't invited either, I take it? I was very embarrassed when I called over. Lunch for two.'

'I'm sure the food was lovely,' Fidelma said.

'I didn't think much of the muck you cooked up for your gentleman caller,' Iris said, turning again to her daughter.

'I've cooked worse,' Gloria said, determined not to rise to the provocation.

'I'm sure the smell went up the lift-shaft to your floor, Fidelma. In any case, he didn't eat much.'

'You drove him away.'

'*He* drove *me* away in his car, if you recall.' Again, she deferred to Fidelma. 'After he disposed of the tree you hacked. The tree Richard had in a pot. I only came to wish Gloria a happy birthday, and to bring her present.'

'Thank you, mother.'

'Did you see it, Fidelma? A lovely cashmere cardigan. She hasn't worn it, have you, dear? You didn't think to wear it for your mad trek?'

'Who has champagne at a funeral reception?' Gloria demanded.

'I do.' Her mother replied. 'You forget we had it for your father.'

'So we did.'

'We were celebrating the life of the departed. Your father. Your husband, Richard. Remember that.'

'You're right.'

'I am? That's good to hear. And, can I say, people drank it.'

'It was a lovely gesture,' Fidelma said. Did she mean serving up the champagne or graciously drinking it? That wasn't clear.

'Actually,' admitted Iris, 'that champagne we had for Richard was rotten. I'll be lodging a complaint with the off-licence. Bloody cheek, offloading that on us.'

'I'll show you my new cardigan in a minute, Fidelma.' The gin was starting to have an effect. Gloria was ready to go with the flow.

'Please. I'd like to see it.'

Iris let out a conciliatory sigh, and gazed into the corner. 'Oh Gloria, you don't want me meddling, I know. You don't want advice from me. You have your own feet and inches, but what is it you *do* want? Company? Well, here we are. And there's many others, if you'd let them call.'

'I'm glad you're here.'

Iris wanted to indulge her daughter. Embarrassment was a reliable short-circuiter. 'If it's sex . . . well, that's not a problem these days. So I hear.'

'She doesn't hear it from me, Fidelma.'

'By the way,' Fidelma came in with a sudden brightness, 'did that woman call?'

'Who?'

'Virginia Coates.'

'Detective Garda Barrett . . . .'

'What?'

'He mentioned Virginia Coates. A childhood friend of Richard's, he said. What does she want?'

Fidelma told her story about meeting Virgina Coates. The woman had called to Gloria's apartment the previous night, had found no one in, had met Fidelma in the lobby, had seen her go across the road to the café, had followed her there. She had introduced herself, and had asked Fidelma if she knew the Meadows, had said she was an old friend of Richard's. She was very sad to hear the news, wanted to speak to Gloria. She wanted information. 'When I told her the Guards were suspicious about the circumstances, she got upset. What did I mean, she wanted to know. That it didn't happen where they found him.'

'You shouldn't be telling strangers such things, Fidelma,' Gloria said, rounding on her friend.

'I'm sorry. She was so concerned. She left in a hurry. She said she would call back.'

'We don't know what happened,' Gloria asserted forcefully.

'Richard was knocked down and killed, Gloria,' Iris cried. 'He's dead, and you haven't told us what he was doing wandering out there. I know what *you* were doing,' she admitted. 'You were atoning. What was *he* doing? Please tell me.'

'I. Don't. Know,' Gloria shouted.

And she didn't.

There was a stark silence. It ran so deep Richard had no presence in it.

Gloria's mother apologised for her outburst. Her desire was to protect her child from all harm. 'I'm sorry,' she said. 'We'll let him go.'

25

Detective Garda Jarleth Barrett pretended to be angry with her. 'Don't you know I would have driven you there if you'd asked me? You should have asked.'

She tried one of his shrugs. That annoyed him. '*Now* look,' he said, pointing to the plaster-cast on her wrist. 'It'll be months before you're right.'

The poor fellow couldn't make his assertion sound credible.

'Have you news?'

'I'm here to see that you're all right.'

'I am. Thank you.'

'You look tired, did the doctor say?'

'Yes. I haven't been sleeping.'

'So you go out and do that to yourself.' He pointed to the plaster-cast.

'You want to come walking with me?' Gloria teased.

'I do not.'

Well, of course he did. 'I'll drive you anywhere you want to go.'

His concern was genuine, no doubt about it. He made her give a detailed account of her pilgrimage. He drilled down until he got her to admit to her expanding programme of night-walks, got her to describe the various routes and timings, was careful not to ask for an explanation. Instead, he did a lot of nodding. 'You want me to go there again with you?' he asked, when she was finished.

'No.'

'It's served its purpose, this walking?'

'I like to roam now.'

'At unsociable hours. Where it isn't safe.'

'I'm getting better at judging.'

'You can't find anyone who'll go with you? Your friend . . . ' – she saw him make a quick search in his mental notebook for the name – 'Fidelma, for instance. No?'

'I want my own company.'

'For now, you say?'

'I'll be careful.'

'Glad to hear it, but I'm not satisfied.'

'You are that concerned? You shouldn't be.'

More nodding. More pointing at the plaster-cast, with the nod turning into a rueful shake.

'You'll stay for a cup of tea?'

'I will not.' He was on to her blocking moves, perhaps.

'I'm making it for myself. You might as well.'

'I've gone off tea.'

'Really? That's unusual.'

He came away from his position by the window and stood in front of her at the arm of the couch. He transferred his weight uneasily from one foot to the other. 'Gloria, you will forgive me – '

She jumped in. 'Will I?' She didn't speak in an aggressive tone. Suppressed alarm, more like, at his heavy use of her name.

'I couldn't help noticing – '

'What?' She was doing what he did, jumping in before the other had finished. She was very annoyed with herself, but she coped.

'Noticing how attractive you are . . . .'

'Oh.' She didn't blush. She just let the alarm ring.

'Yes. Very.'

'Oh.' There was a downward inflection here, to discourage any sudden action.

'Oh yes,' he affirmed earnestly. 'This is not something I've done before.'

'No . . . .'

'You understand?'

'I do.'

'I should wait, perhaps, but I can't.' His speaking out her first name had made him instantly light-headed. 'I don't want you thinking I'm impatient. I'm a patient man, Gloria, but these are exceptional circumstances, you'd agree?'

'Well – '

He didn't let her finish. 'I must seize this opportunity.'

'Seize? In what way?'

'I want to ask now if you are interested?'

'In?'

'Will you take a chance on me . . . with me?' he corrected. He moved closer to her in the brief silence that followed, and tried to encourage a positive response by re-locking eyes with her. He was dancing lightly on his feet. He was having a rush of confidence.

He wanted to reach out and take her hands and squeeze them, but he restrained himself. After all, there was the plaster-cast to consider. 'Is it too much to ask? I don't think it's too much.'

The muscles tightened around Gloria's lips. Her gaze shifted to the corner of the room.

He went ahead. 'Are you shocked? Of course you are. Please don't answer just yet.'

'I'm not shocked. Thank you, Jarleth. We'll talk.'

'I'm going to go now.'

'That would be best.'

Though she attached no real significance to it, she had intended to tell Barrett about Virginia Coates calling, just to be thorough. However, his advances threw her. She would ring him when he was behind his desk. She leaned in and kissed him on the cheek to prevent his lurching. 'Good night.'

'Good night, Gloria. And thank you.'

Barrett left the apartment in a hurry. Gloria raised her plaster-cast in the air and took herself to the window to watch her detective scurry down the street. She had been thanked for cooperating. It was only now that she remembered she had seen Barrett in the courts. Giving evidence in a Traveller case.

He was still in uniform. He was finding it difficult under cross-examination, she recalled, constantly having to refer to his notebook.

Didn't he see here that she was heartbroken?

He did not, though he must have queried it in his notebook.

26

It was late again when Gloria came out of her apartment building and stood on the pavement looking left and right. There was a new balance to be struck with the soles of her walking shoes now that her arm was bound and parcelled. She tested the distribution of weight with a roll of her hips. She rolled one shoulder, then the other. That brought on what felt like a deep thrombotic pain – she imagined the two parts of the broken bone rubbing together like tectonic plates – but it quickly subsided when straightened her spine.

She fully intended to set off on the pavement: east or west, she didn't know which. She was distracted by the scene across the street. There were painters and decorators at work in the café. She could see them through the shutters. There were two of them slapping paint on the walls at an impressive rate. That was good, wasn't it: change?

She stepped to the curb and watched. For no particular reason she stood with her toes extending beyond the edge. She noted that the painters' white van had a slow puncture, rear wheel, left-hand side. She was sure they knew.

When she saw a taxi approaching, she put her hand out.

'Where to?'

'Howth.'

The driver indicated, made a U-turn. 'Howth it is.'

Gloria took her phone out and dialled Tom's number. Tom could see who was calling from his display. *Gloria.*

'Sorry to ring so late. I'm coming over. Is that all right?' She had never been so brazen, not even with her husband. What do you make of this, Richard, my love? The situation is workable, you'd say. Good to follow through. And how brave you are: all sweaty, no make-up, wearing only duds.

'Oh yes, Gloria. Please do come over. I'm up. I'm wide awake.'

'Good. I'll be there in twenty minutes.'

The taxi-driver shook his head. Even with the road clear it would take at least thirty-five minutes. He knew his fare was on a mission – illicit, he thought. Knew she didn't want to talk. Lust was a fine thing. He went heavy on the accelerator pedal. Gloria sat back in the seat and made her limbs go limp. She gazed out the window at the streetlights floating upstream. She let her head empty.

'Good God, Gloria, what did you do to yourself?' Tom brayed when he flung open the door.

'Broke it.' She felt foolish and proud. 'You're not to mind it.'

'Of course I mind it. What on earth did you do?' She gave him a brief and unflattering account of what she had done. Passing across the threshold of the house that was about to be repossessed felt warm and inviting. Tom was looking older and more battered tonight. That was reassuring. Furthermore, he was overwhelmed, in a weary sort of way. Gloria kissed him. 'Do you think we could manage?'

★

They formally thanked each other for the sex they had. Thank you, Gloria. Thank you, Tom. There was no embarrassment, and no immediate regret. The milk in the fridge was sour. Strong black coffee suited both of them. It seemed to go with a slow-moving, uncluttered morning, which they began very early.

'You're anxious to go?' he asked – out of politeness, really.

'I'm already gone,' she replied.

This kind of calm panic was a rare thing in both their lives, and was thrilling. Neither questioned their own actions. They avoided speculating about further intimate encounters. That was for when they were alone and reviewing their separate desires.

'I'll give you a lift.'

She turned the offer down flat. 'I'll walk a little.'

'More walking.' He smiled.

'I want the air.'

He was going to offer to walk with her, any distance, but thought better of it. He was keen to show he was listening. 'More coffee?'

215

PHILIP DAVISON

She kissed him so firmly on the lips that it made him reach around her waist and pull her in to him fiercely.

'I'm gone,' she whispered over his shoulder. Coupling and uncoupling: could it really be this clean and emphatic? She was getting away with it; that was the feeling, but the test didn't apply.

Thank you, Tom. Thank you, Gloria.

Dublin bay was placid, the air sharp, damp and pleasing to her. There was sunlight on the water, the crown of the headland, the top of the tree canopy in the park that came down to the seafront road. A shimmer came from the windscreen of a car on Bull Island, beyond the lagoon. The occupants were out walking the golf course, Gloria imagined, or were on the beach. The early-morning commuters still had a clear run into the city. The click and mock flat-tyre burr from the concrete road assaulted her ears and spurred her on.

Gloria was determined she would make her way home on foot. She lengthened her stride, then broke into a run. The running was unnecessary, exhilarating, and would soon be nauseous, but on she went. Super bag-lady stuff, were she not going

216

back to her apartment to sit and think and plan who else she might bed, and shock poor dead Richard with her grieving.

There were barristers in chambers, and clerks of the court who had the eye for her. At least one judge. That crooked solicitor. There was the man in the fruit-and-veg market she had passed on her way to King's Inns. What was it about him?

Gloria was planning to fit in in a non-conformist way, not jump into a dumpster. The tide was not yet fully in. On the stretch between the East Wall and Clontarf seafront. the silver shadow mudflats seemed to tremor in response to Gloria's pounding feet. She called out to Richard, but he made no appearance. Where was his heart spray? Gone missing in her cleaning frenzy. She called again, but she was hopeful for something else. She didn't know what. What was clear to her was that she had loved, and had been loved. She had shrunk to that part of a human being that cannot be reordered, amended or otherwise changed. Stripped down, bereft of answers, exhausted, she could build again from there. She saw that she would be free to spring forwards when her strength had returned, free to take her chances – which she vowed she would do.

She felt that if she spread her arms and made fairings of her fingertips, the wind would lift her, but there could be no proper arm-spreading for now. The bone-pain was back, now that she was swinging the bunched arm, and she hadn't brought the painkillers she'd been given. In any case, she was sure that if she got airborne she would be blown off course. That was for another day.

But were she to be lifted up and carried across the far arm of the bay, she might have passed over Virginia Coates' mothballed house in Killiney, where, unknown to her, a related scene was playing out. The obsessive John Miller was being confronted by his erstwhile lover. He had been camping in the house waiting for Virginia to return, and now he had his reward. The deluded and angry John would not accept that their stormy affair was over. She had it wrong, she'd see. He didn't care about her new art-school lover. That could be ended in an instant. There was nothing – absolutely nothing – that would see him break with Virginia.

She told him she knew what he had done, and was sickened. He told her he deeply regretted his action, but no part of it could be undone. She got down on the living-room floor with him. Their rutting was hard, unaffectionate and soundless. It made Virginia weep for Richard Meadows and for herself. This was an end, she assured John. She could not live with a man who had committed such an act.

'You'll get away with this, I know,' she declared softly. Those were her parting words. Strangely, they were meant to comfort.

27

Tom rang Gloria, but she didn't answer. He left a message: would she come to Paris with him for a long weekend? They could slip away. He didn't tell her, of course, but he'd gladly use the emergency cash that he kept hidden behind a loose skirting board. It was extraordinarily exciting to him, the prospect of spending the very last reserve, his flit-money, on himself and Gloria. What a way to hit the buffers. It was a proper fait accompli.

Gloria thought she might say yes. Repeat their assignation in Paris. Repeat their clean break. That was no less exciting.

John Miller drove his killer sports car to Donnybrook Garda Station, where he stopped directly outside the entrance, in a bus lane and on double yellow lines. He got out and walked into the desk sergeant in a trance. He made his confession, then went and sat in a corner until he was led to an interview room.

Detective Barrett was called, but at that moment he was on a hospital trolley being wheeled to theatre with acute appendicitis. *Saved by the knife*, Barrett was thinking, his eyes looking down along his body to where the surgeon would cut. Then, back on the job with fresh resolve. *We make the world better piecemeal*, he was thinking. *That's as good as it gets*. He'd have another go at Gloria Meadows. It was the right thing to do. He'd get her father's piano tuned, get her playing again, to lift herself up. In light of the remote possibility that he would not wake from his general anaesthetic, Jarleth Barrett was having a philosophical spurt.

The Richard Meadows case would be dealt with by another, more experienced detective, though that experience would not be needed.

In Donnybrook, a bus-horn sounded, but nobody came out to the car that had been left with the keys in the ignition and its engine running.

Despite prolonged and exhaustive police inter-
views, and sustained pressure from legal counsel,
John Miller resolutely refused to offer any explanation for the killing of Richard Meadows. Nor
would he give details as to the precise location of
the deed. He would only admit to killing Richard
Meadows by running him over, dumping the body
and burning the car. Miller's obsession with
Virginia Coates, the absolute loyalty his love for her
inspired, ensured that her name was not formally
linked to his action. Barrett would later interview
Virginia Coates and establish a connection between
her and Miller. There was, however, no proof of her
knowledge of the incident, and no evidence of her
being complicit.

The case of Michael Tierney, knocked down and
killed by a hit-and-run driver, would go unresolved.